# Hearts Are Like Balloons

### Candace Robinson

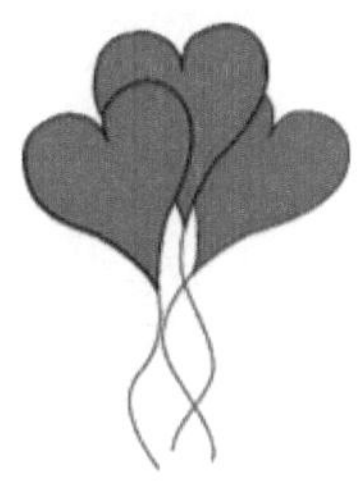

*For my dad*
*See you on the other side*

# Chapter One

♡

"Daddy, how does this look?" I held up my masterpiece—a turtle with only three legs.

He walked from his desk to mine. I was finally able to get me a desk after asking Mommy and Daddy for so long. They said the art room was now complete.

Mommy was busy outside watering flowers, while Daddy would rather work on art with me.

Shuffling to where I was sitting, Daddy's eyebrows rose as he picked up my painting. "Why does it only have three legs?"

Looking down, I puckered my lips and tried to think about it. "I don't know. I saw a dog with three legs. I think it was the other day."

Daddy set down my picture, and it made a crinkling sound as he nodded at me. "Well, I love it. But you shouldn't rush—take your time. You can take a lifetime on this one picture, May, and it would be okay."

I studied my turtle that I chose to color green and yellow only. "But I like how it looks," I whined.

Daddy stared at me and laughed, causing creases at the side of his mouth to form. "It does look beautiful, May, but there's always room for improvement. Let me show you."

Reaching forward, he took a new sheet of paper and grabbed my paintbrush, gradually dipping it into the already-

*soaked watercolor. He painted a few slow strokes across the paper using the same dark green I'd chosen, shaping an outline of a turtle. "Do you see what I'm talking about?"*

*"I did do that!" I cried.*

*Daddy let out another laugh. "Here, let me really show you." He placed the paintbrush in my hand—I clenched it, and then he put my tiny fist between his. Slowly, he moved my hand back and forth across the paper, this time picking out a blue for the inside of the shell. He constantly dipped the brush into other colors, such as purple and pink—using slow, precise strokes to fill in the spaces.*

*His hand stopped moving, and he smiled down at me. "Do you understand now?"*

*I looked at the paper, then back at my masterpiece. They were both three-legged turtles, but this one looked prettier. Mine still had a lot of open space inside the turtle where I missed the color. "I do!"*

Dad's the one who first introduced me to art. I know almost all kids color with crayons, but he showed me more than coloring. He taught me shading and techniques that my tiny brain latched on to. We moved on from coloring and drawing to working with paints, ceramics, and other materials. I learned from him that we could use anything around the house and make it a project.

# Chapter Two

A few days ago, my dad was admitted to the hospital for trouble breathing—he was diagnosed with cancer.

My dad has been sent home to die. That's his sentence. Death. At. Home. Hospice is being sent out to help with anything that he needs. It's a good thing they'll come and help, but then it's a reminder of what's to come next. I don't know what I feel, but it's a mixture of anger, sadness, and numbness.

Two days ago, my mom came into my room with her black hair a disheveled mess. Mom told me she was calling nine-one-one and for me to get ready to go to the hospital because Dad was having trouble breathing. The ambulance arrived and took him, while my mom and I followed the ambulance in her car. Tears constantly ran, smearing Mom's mascara, and I sat there thinking that the hospital would help Dad get better.

We got there, and from one second of looking at my dad, the doctor immediately knew there was something wrong. Hell, anyone would've known there was something wrong. She probably knew the instant she laid eyes on his thin frame that it was cancer. The chest x-ray proved there *was* a tumor in his lungs.

When the doctor said the word tumor, I tried to stay

positive. I kept thinking to myself, *this situation has a light at the end of the tunnel*. He could have surgery and get the tumor out, and everything would go back to how it was two years ago when my dad was still my dad. Hope was still on my side.

Nope. That didn't happen. Dad was carted away several times for tests. Mom had a look of shock spread across her tired face when she heard the cancer had spread to other organs. Dad seemed surprised that it was cancer and had been in denial this entire time.

The devastation was done, and that was that. Cancer had already won. Mission accomplished. My dad's insides were being eaten away until there would be nothing left. The doctors still wanted to probe inside his stomach, but Dad turned them down. I would've, too. If nothing could be done, then why did they want to cut him open?

Dad finished his third blood transfusion when he started to get antsy and asked to head home. His hand would constantly tap the arm rail, and he looked back and forth between Mom and the door with his eyebrows permanently drawn downward. Why was he so anxious to go home? I had never seen Dad like that before, but I understood. I wouldn't want to spend any more time in a hospital, either.

While at the hospital, I people watched, and that place is a sad, sad world. Yes, I saw plenty of newborn babies being carted off to their new homes, but the precious specks of life were overshadowed by all the sickness that surrounded the halls. People were wheeled in, but never wheeled out.

The damn smell of the hospital, a mixture of too many cleaning products combined with sickness, will never fade from my memories.

We finally arrive home and after pulling into the driveway, I hop out and hurry to the passenger side to help Mom get my dad out of the car.

"May, can you grab his cane from inside the house for me?" Mom asks, appearing exhausted from Dad leaning on her. He has been using a cane for a while now after becoming so fragile and weak.

For two years now, my mom and I have known something was wrong with him. He has been dropping a lot of weight—at least sixty pounds. Dad was about two hundred to begin with, and we recently found out he only weighs one-hundred and forty pounds. I knew he'd lost a lot, but I didn't realize it was so significant—maybe it was because I saw him every single day. I noticed how thin he had gotten around six months ago, his arms smaller than mine, and I can't even describe the emotion that consumed me when I first noticed this. It was sorrow mixed with disbelief, making my chest feel hollow.

"Sure. I'll be right back." I unlock the door inside the garage and locate the cane that's propped beside my dad's recliner, as if waiting for its owner to return. The dragon head on top seems to be mocking me.

Stupid cane. I want to take it and break it in half over my knee and burn the remains to ashes.

When my parents had me, Dad was older, but I feel like he's still too young to use a walking stick.

Gently, I carry the wooden cane to my mom, and I try to soften my angry thoughts. It isn't like the cane knows what I'm thinking since it's wood and all, but I still feel bad about being so angry. After all, it has helped my dad get around when he couldn't walk on his own.

When I return to the garage and close the door behind me, I can smell cigarette smoke. *Please tell me my dad isn't already lighting up a cigarette?* But I know better than to think that because cigarettes have been a top priority, even more so since he's been sick.

I stomp directly up to him. "Dad, you can't be serious, can you?" I hand the cane to my mom, who is sitting next to my dad in a ratty fold-up lawn chair that should be thrown in the trash.

They're both seated at the small, wooden table that my dad made a long time ago. Over the last few weeks, he has used it to play solitaire, solve puzzles, or create his artwork.

"May, if I want to have a cigarette, I'm going to have one, okay?" Dad peers at me with a tired expression and then back toward the table where a partially finished puzzle sits next to his sketchpad.

His green eyes are missing the miraculous glow that used to be there. Now they're dim and faded, losing all their shine.

"You heard what the doctors said, and you shouldn't be smoking anyway. You should've quit a long time ago when I begged you to." I point at Mom. "Like she asked you."

He has been playing the on and off game of smoking cigarettes his entire life. There has been a remarkably higher number of *on* moments.

I pushed and pushed for my dad to go to the doctor to see what was going on. I even told my mom to make him get a checkup. Mom tried, but when he said no, she said that was his choice. I don't understand why my dad has always been against going to the doctor. She cried every day, knowing something was wrong with him, and I wish she would've put her foot down and made him go. I, on the other hand, had the optimistic attitude of believing it was something that could be straightened out with medication—that it was a misunderstanding or something easy to fix. Why he wouldn't go doesn't make any sense to me at all. My dad's always been a mystery and kept his thoughts to himself—he's a book of blank pages that needs magic to make the words appear. *Why wouldn't he just go to the doctor?*

"Look, for whatever time I have left, I'm going to do what helps me relax. Got it?" he snaps.

Tears well up in my mom's eyes as she glances in my direction. "Can you head inside and make us some lunch?"

Maybe I shouldn't, but I blame my mom as much as I do my dad for not pressuring him to see the doctor sooner. For whatever stubborn reason, I know he wouldn't have done the chemo treatments if he had gone sooner anyway.

"Sure, Mom."

Searching Dad's face one more time, I shake my head and walk toward the door. I take the knob in my hand and slam it as hard as I can behind me, the sound reverberating throughout the house. I don't feel the slightest bit bad for rattling the walls.

Grabbing the loaf of bread, I inspect the printed date and notice it expired a couple of days ago. When I examine the bread, it's mold free, so I grab the ham and cheese, adding mayo to my dad's sandwich with a little bit of lettuce. Mom likes hers with mustard and fully loaded with lettuce. I normally load up on multiple condiments for myself.

After I finish making the sandwiches, I bring them outside to my parents and sit beside Dad. He's already sketching flowers in one of his drawing pads—it's obviously for my mother, since she has been infatuated with any kind of flower for as far back as I can remember.

Mom stuffs a bite of sandwich into her mouth, then sets it down. She brushes her hands together and watches the crumbs fall to the ground like pieces of snow. "Thank you for making the sandwiches, sweetheart."

The anger that has built inside me over Dad's refusal to seek help withered after he received his diagnosis. Now I'm nothing but a hollow void sitting and waiting to be filled back in with a shovel. My emotions have always been able to understand things in a way where people might consider them robotic. I still cry and get upset, but I know I'll be able to heal from this quicker than most.

"You're welcome," I reply to her, then look at Dad's sandwich that has two small bites taken out of it. "Aren't you going to finish that, Dad?"

He gives me a half smile, but it's missing anything real—it's false advertisement for happiness. "I'll save the rest for later."

We both know he won't finish the sandwich—his appetite has been non-existent these past six months from being sick. With the news he received, he probably doesn't care about food.

I decide to head inside to call my best friend Jessie, who has been texting me non-stop over the past couple of days. I could text her back, but sometimes you just need to talk to the person on the phone. She's one of the only people I can really confide in.

The couch is already calling my name, and I crash into the soft cushions, pulling the disheveled, fleece blanket from the corner over my legs. Scrolling through my recent calls, I click on Jessie's name.

After two rings, she answers. "May?"

Huffing long and loud, I hear my frustration echo into the phone. "Hey, Jess. Sorry it took me so long to get back to you."

"No, no," she rushes. "Don't worry about it. What's going on? How's your dad? Do you need anything? I know I'm already playing the question game, and you've probably had enough questions to last a lifetime."

A small snort escapes me. "You have no idea, Jess. First, Dad does have cancer, and second, talking to you will help me right now."

I break it down from the beginning for her—she already knew Dad was taken to the hospital by ambulance for trouble breathing, but that's as far as I got. I tell her everything from finding the tumor to there being nothing we can do.

"He has basically been sent home to die," I sob.

I hadn't cried this entire time, until now. I don't want to lose my dad. We don't talk a lot, but we don't really have to. I understand him, and he understands me, and I love him so much.

Dad and I may not have had a lot of conversation, but we did a lot of things growing up besides art, too. I remember after Dad would get home from work when I was younger, we'd solve puzzles. Except I'd gather about fifteen puzzles and empty them all out into one big pile. We would then split the puzzles and try to find all the pieces to match up to their picture.

There was even a time when I collected tons of those rubber bouncy balls, and we would invent games using those.

To me, it was the best experience, and I have to hold onto that.

Those small details I haven't thought about in years, and I don't want to forget them, either. I admire him in so many ways.

"Do you want me to come over?" Jessie asks.

I do want her to come over, but I want to spend time with my dad today. "How about tomorrow?"

"You got it, girlie. Let me know the time, and I'll be there five minutes before."

This is true. She always arrives exactly five minutes before she's expected anywhere. "Okay, how about noon?"

Jessie agrees that will work, and I end the phone call. I walk back to the garage to see how my parents are doing, and they're already halfway to the door.

I'm a child who still believes in miracles and that life will find its way back to normality. It's two weeks until I turn seventeen, and that's two weeks until nothing changes. What was I hoping for anyway? Maybe to wake up to Dad being okay. A birthday is just another day. I guess I was kidding myself thinking that a birthday wish could cure my dad's cancer.

"Your father wants to come in and rest in front of the TV for a while," Mom says.

I hold the door open for them, and Dad slowly walks to the recliner, carefully lowering himself to the seat.

"Jana, can you grab me a water out of the fridge?" Dad asks.

"I'll get it." I speed walk to the fridge, pull one out and hand it quickly to my dad, as if he's going to dehydrate. Staring at him, I can see he's completely exhausted from the short walk inside. He's winded, and small beads of perspiration rest above his brow.

"Thanks, May," Mom and Dad say simultaneously. They both let out small laughs, and I can't help it, a smile tugs at my lips. The moment may be a strange time for smiles, but it comes nonetheless. Then a tiny storm of coughs triggers and unloads from Dad's chest. Rushing over to Dad, Mom props him forward, striking his back several times with the palm of her hand. The sounds stop, and he leans back in the chair, letting out a long sigh.

We watch TV for a bit after that, and Mom constantly glances at Dad with worry.

Dad studies Mom and me with a blank expression. "I think I need to go and rest for a while in bed." He didn't get much sleep at the hospital, so I understand completely.

"Sure, Eugene. Rest as long as you need," Mom says.

Dad tries to stand up, but he falls right back into the recliner. He tries again and falls back down once more, frustration growing on his face by the second. Mom reaches him before I do and helps him out of the chair.

"Here, let me help you." Taking hold of his arm, Mom pulls him up to stand. His weakness has consumed him, and I feel helpless for not knowing what to do.

Leaving my seat to walk over to Dad, I wrap my arms around his waist before he walks to his room. My stomach drops in an instant from not being able to feel anything but his bones. "Goodnight, Dad."

"Goodnight." His voice comes out raspy. Mom takes him to their room, holding onto him with everything she has.

The phone rings while Mom is still in the bedroom, so I

walk to the kitchen table where her cell phone is still safely tucked inside her purse. I hurry to pull the phone out and look at the name of the caller. It's my Uncle Jim. *Maybe I shouldn't answer it,* I think. He'll ask too many questions I don't have answers to, but then I change my mind. After all, he is my dad's brother.

"Hello."

"Hey, this must be May." Before I have a chance to answer, he continues to talk. "Is Eugene around?"

I've seen Uncle Jim twice in my whole life. He lives in Arizona, and I really don't know a lot about him other than he calls my dad maybe twice a year. Those days would be the usual birthday and Christmas—the other times my mom has to do the calling.

"You just missed him, Uncle Jim. He went to lie down." Slowly, I drag my hand down my face, not wanting to talk about Dad. It will only cause tears to spring from my eyes, and I had enough of that earlier on the phone with Jessie. There will be oceans upon oceans of tears to follow once Dad is gone.

"Well, can I speak to Jana then?" he asks. I sigh in relief that I can avoid further conversation—Uncle Jim is always awkward on the phone, and I don't feel like dealing with that at the moment.

A rustling and soft squeak comes from my parents' bedroom as I hear Mom close the door. "Let me get her. I hear her heading out of the bedroom."

Mom walks into the living room, and I hold the phone out for her to take. I mouth that it's Uncle Jim, and she looks up at the ceiling with a "not now" expression. But she manages to take the phone from my hand with a look of exhaustion mixed with frustration. For the most part, he sits in silence with me on the phone, but when he talks to Mom, he rambles on about nothing. Maybe I should've told him she was busy.

She probably thinks it's better to talk to him now instead of later because he *will* call back. Ever since he heard about Dad going to the hospital, he keeps calling to check in on him.

Turning on the TV, I half pay attention to it and half eavesdrop on the phone call. Mom is sitting at the kitchen table sharing the details with him. He doesn't seem to understand, and she has to repeat the story again. Mom didn't want to give him all the details until they knew exactly what was going on because she knew he'd get all worked up.

She's in the middle of telling Uncle Jim about hospice coming out soon to help with Dad, when a loud *boom* echoes from my parents' bedroom. My entire body freezes and molds into the couch, too afraid to move.

# Chapter Three

$\heartsuit$

What was that sound from Dad's bedroom? My body shakes like mini volcanoes erupting. Slowly, my head turns toward Mom, who is still busily explaining the situation on the phone.

"Did you hear that noise from the bedroom?" I ask, nervously.

Her forehead wrinkles in confusion. "No?" Mom hurries to tell my uncle that she'll have to call him back and rushes to the bedroom.

I don't know how she didn't hear that sound—it had to have been a gunshot. Jitters fly throughout my body, and I'm too scared to walk to their bedroom. I feel like a coward, but I don't want to see what I already know.

Before I finally decide to help my mom in their bedroom, she rushes out. "May, go outside now. I have to call an ambulance."

I want to argue, but I don't. Running to the door, I leave the house with shaky hands and shock setting in. Tears form, and I try to keep them from streaming down my face.

*Why would he do this?* I walk and sit on the bench in our front yard and wait for my mom.

Mom comes outside, panicked. "I called the ambulance,

and they're coming. May, I think he's gone."

"Why? Why would he do this?"

She shakes her head. "He just fell."

I stare at her. "What do you mean fell? I heard that noise, and it sounded like a gunshot." There's no way that was him falling.

Her eyes whip to mine. "I didn't hear anything. There was blood on his head, but I think he fell. Let me go back in and check."

She starts for the door, and I grab her arm to pull her back. "Wait for the ambulance. Going back in there will only make things worse."

We're both panicked and not sure what to do. Mom wants to fight me on this and confirm what I already know—but at least she didn't hear the shot. Mom has a way of shutting out sounds, but I can't believe she didn't hear it.

The ambulance arrives, followed by several fire trucks and numerous police cars. A female officer speed walks to where we are. She has light brown skin and long, black hair pulled into a low ponytail. "What happened?" the officer asks. "Is there anyone else inside?" Her expression is neutral with all emotion safely tucked away behind her tightly pressed lips. It makes me uncomfortable, and I feel like I'm talking to a cyborg.

"I don't know what happened," Mom cries. "I thought he fell, but now my daughter is telling me she heard a gunshot." I stand completely still beside her and nod.

A male cop rushes inside the house. The screen door slams, and it seems like forever before he finally comes back out, confirming what I knew. My dad shot himself in the head.

I plop down on the wooden bench in our front yard, not crying, but trembling from the spontaneous way everything went down. My dad was just here, and I didn't even have a chance to say goodbye. It doesn't feel real. My emotions are pure shock, more than anything else.

Mom is sitting beside me in tears. The bright, yellow caution tape is being wrapped around the front of the house where my parents' bedroom is located. It's like a beacon calling all the neighbors to take a gander.

Everywhere I look, there are people staring at what's going on at our house. Nosy neighbors are standing outside of their houses staring our way. Cars are slowing down as they pass to get a glance of what's happening. I want to turn the hands of the clock backward and go back in time.

Brown paper bags are being placed on our hands. "Why do we have to have these on?" Mom asks. All the bags do is make me feel confined and confused.

"It's standard procedure until the detective arrives," the female officer says.

While watching my mom, I want to console her, but I can't get my emotions in check. It's as if I'm watching myself from somewhere else, and I'm not really present. But I still manage to get words out. "They have to confirm we don't have any gunpowder on our hands. You know, to make sure we didn't have anything to do with this."

"Do we have to really sit here on display for the entire neighborhood to observe? I want my husband back. I want to talk to Eugene," Mom sobs.

She can't even lift her hands to her face with the bags hiding them, so she covers her eyes with her inner elbow and lets out small sniffles.

When the EMTs wheel my dad out, I close my eyes the entire time. They're clenched so tight to make this seem like a dream—when it isn't. I know he's going to be covered, but I can't look at it—I can't look at him. My dad underneath a bedsheet isn't what I want my final memory of him to be. But I still hear the roll of the wheels, and the pounding from the paramedics' shoes against pavement.

Mom's much stronger than me in a lot of ways. I couldn't even go in the room to help her. After already having to remember Dad in his thin state from the cancer that ate him inside out, I didn't want to have this memory embedded in my brain either.

Continuing to keep my eyes closed, I try to think of happier times. Mom wraps her arm around my shoulders, and the warmth is constricting, but I don't shove it away. "He's already in the ambulance. You can open your eyes now."

Lifting my head, I open my eyes but still avoid looking at the ambulance. The motor eventually starts and pulls away.

A detective arrives, and the bags are taken off our hands—where there happens to be no gunpowder. I could've told them that, but I understand it's their job.

He's a small, bald man that seems genuinely nice. "Is it okay if I ask you some questions? I'll take you to my car, if that's alright?"

Mom peers at him and barely nods. "Okay." Her tears have stopped, and I think she's feeling the shock now, too.

While I'm watching Mom in the car, our neighbor Mrs. Jenkins, pulls onto the street. Her driveway is blocked by the police vehicles, so she parks next to the curb.

She takes one look at me when she gets out of the car and runs over. The female cop tries to wave her away as she's done with other neighbors, but I tell her it's okay. Mrs. Jenkins' gray hair is properly pulled back into a tight bun on the top of her head. "May, what is going on here?"

I can only shake my head, feeling slightly numb. "My dad isn't here anymore. He shot himself." Tears form in her eyes. Mrs. Jenkins isn't just a neighbor to us, she's like a grandmother to me and much more to Mom. Her wrinkled arms wrap around me, and I just leave mine plastered at my sides, not wanting to hold onto anyone—even though I've known her my entire life.

Opening the door of the police car, Mom walks back to where we are and talks to Mrs. Jenkins. The detective comes up to me next and hands me his card. "If you or your mom need anything, don't hesitate to give me a call. As a person who has struggled with cancer, I get it. Cancer is tough, both physically and emotionally. I know you'll be questioning and questioning, but you can't do that to yourself. This was nothing that you or your mom did."

Swallowing deeply, I let his words sink in and shove his card into my pocket. "Thank you, sir."

He nods and walks back to his car. I don't know how they all do this on a day-to-day basis. My respect for all these workers has increased, and I know I wouldn't be able to do it.

After everyone leaves, a few more neighbors come to the house and talk to my mom outside. They try to comfort her and give me side hugs. *What's with all the touching?* Mom doesn't seem to mind it, but I don't want to be touched right now. I'm not a touchy person in general, only with people I'm close to. But I don't even want to be touched by Mom or Mrs. Jenkins—I want to be alone.

"Do you two want to stay at my house? You can stay as long as you need to," Mrs. Jenkins says, looking at my mom with an expression full of sorrow.

Mom shakes her head sadly. "I can't. I can't stay right next door tonight. I appreciate the offer more than you know, but we're going to have to get a hotel." Relief washes over me when she says this, because I don't want to stay the night anywhere on this street tonight. I'm not grasping everything, but I do understand the whys and the hows, even though the whole situation is unsettling.

Mrs. Jenkins tries a few more times to get us to stay the night. When Mom still refuses, she gives Mom one more long hug. Before Mrs. Jenkins leaves, she says, "Let me know if you change your minds."

Mom turns to me, attempting to hide her thoughts. "Do you want me to grab some things for you, sweetie?" she asks, looking determined to get what she needs from inside our house. I don't want to go back in, but at that moment, I want to be strong like her.

Once inside the house, I avoid glancing at my parents' room. I grab my duffel bag and stuff it with clothing, things from the bathroom, and some snacks from our small kitchen. I don't think I'll be able to eat anything, but Mom might want something.

There's a lingering want to force myself to look at my parents' room on the way out, but I just can't bring myself to do it. I load my bag in the trunk of the car and take a seat in the front, waiting for Mom.

I slide my phone out of my back pocket and stare at it for a while. My fingers need to call Jessie, but my brain doesn't want to work or relay messages to my mouth. I promise myself I'll call her tomorrow.

Finally, Mom walks to the car, her face streaked with new tears.

"Mom, do you want me to drive?" I don't have my license yet, even though I should've gotten it almost a year ago when I turned sixteen.

Reaching over, Mom gives me a kiss on the head. "No, sweetie, I can handle it."

I wish we had more family here. Yes, our neighbor Mrs. Jenkins is like family, but I wish I had a relative who didn't live on our street. My mother's parents both died before I was born, and she didn't have any siblings. The only family Dad has left is Uncle Jim, and he lives in Arizona. It's only a couple of states over from Texas, but it isn't close enough for him to drive. I'm also certain he doesn't have the money to fly here either.

As we pass by several run-down hotels, there are no sounds in the car—only the engine humming along, and neither one of us chooses to turn on the radio. I interrupt the silence that has enveloped us by pointing at a motel in need of a paint job. "Mom, please don't make us stay there."

"We can't afford to stay at an expensive one," Mom replies. Silently, I sit back, and she drives on. Luckily, we agree on the next hotel we come across. It isn't a dump, but it isn't high class either. The paint's still intact, and it doesn't look like it's due for a drug raid.

Sunlight is slowly dimming as we step out of the car,

and I slam the door harder than I meant to. The hotel lobby smells odd when we walk inside—a mixture of dirty carpet with orange-scented Lysol, but the old carpet is overpowering the citrus scent.

A clerk at the front desk is a man in his mid-forties, and he doesn't seem to care about his job by the way he stays staring at his phone when we walk in. He doesn't set his phone down until we're standing at the front desk directly across from him. Any other time I may have given him a smart-alecky comment, but today I don't.

He shoots us a fake smile—all teeth. "Can I help you?" he asks.

"Yes, we need a room," Mom says, giving him a false smile back.

Walking away from their conversation, I see a wall of pamphlets of things to do in our city. I pull one out for the art museum that catches my attention, flipping through it briefly before putting it back. I love art more than anything, but at this moment it only reminds me of Dad. I try not to think about Dad, because then all I can think about is the sound of that gunshot.

"Ready, sweetheart?" I didn't hear Mom's silent steps as she approached.

"Yes."

We take the elevator to the second floor, and the smell is slightly better than downstairs—only Lysol here. Mom stops in front of room 212, and I halt beside her. She unlocks the door with the keycard that has a brown stain across it. Hopefully, this unidentifiable spot isn't from something gross.

Our room is clean enough, so I drop my bag directly in

front of the twin bed on my right and fall down on it, shoes and all. There's a small TV at the center of the room with a green, cloth chair in the corner.

"Sweetie, do you want to talk about it?" Mom asks.

No. I really don't want to talk about anything right now. "Mom, I only want to lie down and go to sleep."

The tears have left Mom's cheeks, but her eyes are bloodshot, and her face is red. "You're going to have to try and eat something, May. You didn't eat lunch."

My appetite is a disaster right now. Nausea fills my stomach, and no matter what I try to eat, I know it won't stay down.

Sitting up, my gaze locks on Mom's. "How about after I shower?"

Mom's eyebrows lower as far down as they'll go, but she nods anyway. "Okay, but when you get out, you're eating."

Grabbing a pair of pajamas from my bag, I walk into the bathroom. The room is so white. Walls, countertop, floor, tub—it's all white. Suddenly, it's like I'm back at the hospital where everything was this exact color—the shade of cleanliness and hidden torture.

The bathroom is surprisingly nice besides the color. I tug off my shirt, followed by the rest of my clothing. Turning on the shower, I step back from the cold blast of water and try to block out the day by thinking about anything else. I scrub and rinse my hair and body three times to make it all disappear, but it doesn't.

Hot water pelts my skin, and I don't mind that it's going to leave it red. I sit down in the shower, resting my back against the slick wall and let the day burn away. Earthquakes rack through my body as I finally cry. I attempt to hold it all in so Mom doesn't hear me, but I can't anymore. Dad has barely been gone, but in this moment, I need him more than ever to get back to myself.

Tears continue to flow down my cheeks, mixing with the shower drops, and I cry until there are no more tears left.

Standing up after I finish, I press my hand against the silver shower knob and imagine I'm stepping out as a new person.

Slowly, I pad to the rectangular, slightly fogged mirror. The new me looks exactly the same. Dark brown hair rests at my neck right above my shoulders, dripping water on my pale skin and causing me to shiver. Green eyes stare back at me from the mirror—the one thing I have that are Dad's. I wish I could somehow claw them out.

After I dress and leave the bathroom, I find Mom sitting on the edge of her bed, talking on the phone with someone. "Yes. You can come out tomorrow, then? How much will it be? Okay, that sounds good."

"Who was that?" I ask as she hangs up the phone.

She gazes at me, then back at her phone and wipes at her blue eyes. "Oh, a cleaning company." Mom pauses. "Do you want to talk about it now, May? We haven't discussed how you feel."

"Mom, I'm not fine today, but I *will* be okay." I let my gaze stay connected with hers because I want her to see I'm telling the truth.

Mom swipes at more tears on her freckled cheeks. "You're old enough, and if and when you have questions, I'll answer them the best I can." My hands shake, but I nod anyway.

Sleepiness hits me, and I want to close my eyes and escape.

I lie down on my bed, but not before Mom hands me a breakfast bar. "At least eat this for me, please?"

Food isn't something I want to think about, but I force it down because I don't need her to worry about anything else. I feel worse for my mom than for myself—he was my dad, but he was her North Star.

Folding the covers back, I slide under the white sheets. The pillow may be a little hard to my liking, but the bed feels like a cloud. Both of us attempt to watch TV, and when that fails, I try to sleep. The last thing I hear before I drift off is Mom sobbing softly.

# Chapter Four

♡

The next day, I call Jessie after waking up. She answers the phone groggily. "Hey."

I grip the phone in my hand with firm pressure. "Look, I know it's early, but can you come over? It's important."

I managed to sleep through the night fine, but when I woke up my chest felt tight as soon as I remembered what my father had done the day before.

"Yes, I can come right over. Is your dad okay?" She sounds fully alert now.

My grip on the phone becomes tighter if that's even possible. "No, Jessie. He isn't."

"Be right there."

"No, wait!" I yell before she can hang up and give her directions to the hotel.

Laying my phone on the bed, I hurry and get dressed. Mom left not long ago to meet up with the cleaning crew and let them in the house. She also wanted to see Mrs. Jenkins, most likely for someone to talk to about my dad. Mom felt guilty that she didn't put away the gun, but she had no idea. Dad used to be positive about everything. Yes, he had looked tired lately and not himself, but he never complained or anything, until he had to go to the hospital a few days ago.

The gun was a small revolver that wasn't even loaded, and it wasn't directly beside the bed either. Dad had to get up and walk to the dresser across from the bed to pull it out of a drawer. He could barely walk when he got home, so I don't even know how he made it to the dresser without me hearing him. He must have used the bed as leverage to hold himself up. Mom can't blame herself, though—she did everything she could've done for Dad by taking care of him.

If I could express my emotions better, I would've tried to comfort Mom more this morning. She let me stay in our hotel room because I told her I wanted to talk to Jessie. It took a while to convince her, but she finally agreed. I want to be there for my mom, but it's uncomfortable right now to be around her. I think if I express how I feel, it will only make matters worse.

The one person I need to see is Jessie. I snack on a blueberry muffin that Mom brought me back from one of the vending machines she found down in the lobby. While I didn't feel like eating yesterday, today my stomach needs it. Right when I'm on my last bite, there's a knock at the door. "Who is it?" Mom told me before she left to not let anyone in unless it was Jessie, and to make sure I asked at the door before answering it.

"It's me!" As soon as I hear Jessie's voice, I unlock the door and wave her inside.

"What's going on here? Why are you at a hotel? Where are your parents? Are you running away?" Her brown eyes roam back and forth across the room, and her blonde hair is swinging all over the place.

My eyebrows shoot up. "What? No! Where would I even be running without a job and money?"

Jessie throws her hands up in the air. "I don't know. There are way younger kids than us who run away all the time."

"Well, I'm not. It's … it's my dad. He died yesterday." My lip quivers and my body starts to shake.

Jessie stares at me with her mouth wide open. "What do you mean *died?* He got released yesterday, right? I know you told me it was terminal, but there's no way it could've happened this soon. Could it?" She stutters on the last two words while tears build in her eyes, because she's known my dad since she was seven.

There's no way to sugarcoat it. "He couldn't take it anymore, Jessie. He shot himself." I feel strange saying it, and I still can't quite grasp it.

"Oh, my God! Why?" she shouts. "Why would he do that? Why would he?" Swinging a hand up to cover her mouth, she lets the tears flow from her face to her shirt, and then onto the hotel carpet.

"I think he couldn't take that he had cancer, and he didn't want to watch himself deteriorate anymore. He saw my grandpa go through hospice, and even though they are there to help, you're watching yourself break apart into smaller pieces, day by day. You see yourself waiting to die until you become nothing. There was no note or anything that he left us," I sob. Mom explained to me this morning why she thought he had shot himself, and the words hospice and cancer triggered it. She isn't even mad he did it—she's more upset he was going to die anyway.

"Do you want to come over to my house, or I can drive us somewhere?" Jessie sits on the bed with her lips drawn down, continuously swiping at the edges of her brown eyes.

I locate my phone on the wooden nightstand. "Let me call my mom to let her know."

Mom answers her phone right away, sounding so sad. "Sweetheart, are you alright?"

"I'm the same. Mom, is it alright if I go to Jessie's house? She's here at the hotel already." I take the stiff hotel pillow and set it in my lap, rubbing my fingers across the edges.

"Go ahead, baby. I have a lot of things to situate, and I need to plan the funeral. If you want me to pick you up, I can come right away," she sniffs. I know as soon as she gets off the phone with me, she's going to have a breakdown with Mrs. Jenkins. A tight ball lands inside my chest—I'm good at internalizing, dealing with my emotions differently than Mom.

"Okay, Mom. Is there anything I can do to help?" Even if she needs me to just sit with her, I will.

"No, not right now. I have to call and make arrangements in a little while. That's it. The clean-up crew already started on the house. They have to cut out a large chunk of the carpet, and I have to throw away the sheets. They'll be finished today, and I thought we could return here next week. Unless you need longer? I want to take a little time away to absorb everything."

"No, Mom, that's fine." I need the space away from home as much as she does.

I don't have a problem with going back to the house, but I already know I won't be able to set foot in the art room for a long time. That's the place where Dad and I spent most of our time together. Mom would come in there, too, and watch us in there for hours. She didn't get bored watching, even though she never joined in.

"I love you, sweetheart." She chokes back another sob.

"Love you, Mom." I hang up the phone first, setting it down beside me and wiping a tear that has made it midway down my cheek.

I turn to Jessie, who is studying me with her lips pressed together. "Are you ready? I ask.

"I'm ready if you are." Reaching over, she rubs my shoulder. Jessie is the one person that I always feel comfortable around. I nod and we walk out of the room.

Jessie speeds to her house, but that's normal for her. Both of her parents are home when we walk inside her cozy house. Her twin brothers aren't in the living room, so that means they're probably in their room playing a video game.

Jessie's mom, Sefina, knows something is wrong by the look on my face. She's from Samoa, and her dark, short hair frames her heart-shaped face. Jessie inherited her beautiful skin color, but got her blonde hair from her dad. Sefina hurries over to me, and I tell her everything that happened yesterday.

She throws her arms around me—more hugging, but with Sefina, it doesn't bother me as much. "You can stay as long as you need to with us, May. That wouldn't be a problem at all."

"Thank you," I say, "but we'll be going back to the house in a week, and Mom already paid for the hotel anyway. Plus, I want to stay with my mom and not leave her by herself because I know she wouldn't want to stay at anyone's house." Mom loves Sefina, but the house would be crowded with us here. Personally, I think I'd also be more comfortable with fewer people.

My mind is buzzing all over the place. Dad worked from home and did graphic design stuff from there. I heard Mom this morning when she was on the phone with Mrs. Jenkins, telling her she's a little worried about not having Dad's income anymore. She'd said the house had been paid off a few years back, which I already knew because my parents got the house right before I was born and did a fifteen-year loan instead of the traditional thirty-year loan. I remember the day specifically when it was paid off because Mom ran out and got us pizza to celebrate. She'd let me pick as many toppings as I wanted, not the usual one topping.

Heading into Jessie's room, I turn around to face her. "Jessie, I know it's soon to ask this, but are you guys going to be hiring at your work anytime soon?"

She nods. "Yeah, we're always hiring. People seem to come and go, while a few others have stuck around. Are you sure you don't want to hold off on it?"

I don't. I'm thinking ahead as I sit in the office chair at her desk. "No. I want to be there to help pay for my stuff, so Mom doesn't have to worry about me more than she already has to."

Jessie cocks her head and runs a finger across her chin. "If you want to, you can apply online and put the start date for when you feel you'll be ready. I'll talk to Violet. I'm sure she won't let me down." Walking to the laptop, she opens it to turn it on.

I lean my head against the back of the chair. "Thanks for helping me."

"That's what friends are for." She types in the web page, pulling up the application form for me to fill out.

Jessie has been my best friend since first grade, and I hated her at first. That was probably the first and only time I actually hated someone.

The first day of class, I had on the most awesome troll shirt I had ever seen. I was so proud of it—it felt like it was a trophy. We were standing in the line for recess, and Jessie turned around, looked at my shirt and grabbed it in her tiny fist. The hair on the troll shirt was made of foamy material, so when Jessie fisted it, her nails left little tiny moon-like indentions.

Sobbing, I'd ran to the teacher. Mrs. Anderson had no idea what was going on. I explained to her what had happened, and she looked at me like I had lost my mind, telling me to get back in line. Sulkily, I walked to the back of the line and thought the rest of the day about how my shirt was ruined, even though the indentions faded throughout the day. I was still mad at the little blonde-haired girl.

A week passed by, and when we were outside at recess, I was climbing on top of this piece of cave-like equipment that I loved so much. Three girls from my class sat underneath, all hidden and talking about ponies—one of them was Jessie. She looked up at me and told me to go away, that I wasn't wanted there with them. I think she was still mad that I told the teacher on her.

When Mrs. Anderson blew her whistle to signal recess was over, the little girls ran out from the cave. Jessie stood up too soon, bumped her head, and started crying. The two other girls looked at her and ran off. I wanted to run off, too, but I didn't.

"Are you okay?" I asked.

"Noooo," she wailed. And that's when our friendship began.

She started following me around in class, then I would

follow her around. We'd get in trouble all the time for talking, and constantly had to be separated on opposite sides of the classroom.

After I finish filling out the application, Sefina makes us chicken alfredo for lunch. Any other day I would scarf this stuff down, but I can barely eat. I force myself to finish the noodles but scoot the chicken to the side of the plate.

I stay until around five, and then Jessie drops me off at the hotel. "Call me if you need anything, okay?" she says. A crease is set so deep between her eyebrows that I don't know if it will go away.

"Don't worry, I'll be bugging you over text tonight." I'll need the distraction from being cooped up in that tiny hotel room.

As I yell bye to Jessie, I walk inside and back to the room.

Mom appears frustrated as she attempts to read a book in bed.

"What are you reading?" I ask softly and sit on the other twin bed.

She shows me the front of the book, and it says something about inspiration. "You know, I don't know what this book is even trying to say. Mrs. Jenkins gave it to me to read to help with things. Maybe it's because I'm not a big reader, but I feel like the writer makes up loads of crap in this book. Most of these writers, have they ever been through anything in real life?"

I study the terrible picture on the cover—a person flying through a finish line. "Maybe? Is that book about running a marathon?"

"No. The picture on the cover doesn't even make sense!"

She tosses the book on the carpet, and I let out a small smile despite everything.

"Anyway, I got it all situated and signed the paperwork for the body to be released to the funeral home. The funeral is going to be in two days." She sighs.

"Alright." It's the only thing I can think of to say. I wish I could rewind every minuscule detail to not just early yesterday, but when all this started happening with Dad. I would've tried with all my power to get him to go to the doctor, harder than I attempted to before. Both of his parents died from cancer, and maybe that affected him more than I thought it did.

"I'm lost. This whole situation is beyond me, so I don't know if you need someone to talk to." She moves to sit next to me on my bed—the mattress dips down, and she leans in close to me.

"Like a counselor?" The thought scares me to talk to someone about my feelings in such detail.

"Yes, sweetheart. You're almost seventeen, and you know your brain better than I do. You've always acted more grown up than you are. If you need me or someone to talk to, I need to know. I'm sure I'll need someone to get me through this." She tiredly rubs her hand across one of her eyes.

I clasp my hands together in my lap. "No. I think if it would've happened out of nowhere, and I didn't understand the reason, I would. I mean, his death was spontaneous, and as much as I wish he wouldn't have shot himself, I get now why he did it. He couldn't handle the situation." If I truly felt I needed a counselor, I would let Mom know.

Slowly, Mom nods. "I'm going to keep my eye on you,

May. If I notice anything change, you're going. But you'll need to at least talk to me about how you feel." She pauses and takes in a deep breath. "And if you need someone more than talking to me, I want you to be honest with me, okay? Even if it's a year from now, you let me know, understand?" She gives me a long hug before sitting back on her bed.

I get up and move to sit beside her because I think she needs me more than I need her at this moment. She orders room service, and after we eat dinner, we sit together on the bed and watch TV as a distraction. When Mom falls asleep, I put my phone on silent and text Jessie for a while, until I drift off to escape.

# Chapter Five

♡

It has been a total of three weeks since Dad died. Being back home these last two weeks is completely different. The hotel was fine, but it wasn't home. Mom complained about how much the cleaning crew over-charged to take care of my parents' bedroom, but in instances like these, they can do what they want. Not a lot of people want to clean blood and whatever else is left behind.

I have been warring back and forth with myself, understanding why he did it and then mad that he did it. I want my dad back, not only for me but mostly for my mom. I'm able to process this situation easier than most, and it may come off as unsympathetic that I don't cry more than I do, but it doesn't mean I'm a hundred percent okay. Death has just always been a part of life for me, and I'm struggling mostly with the sudden aspect of Dad's suicide.

My parents were together for twenty years, and my mom was only twenty when she met my dad. They were standing in line at a fast food restaurant when Dad told her she was the prettiest woman he had ever seen and asked for her number. It may have been an everyday meeting, but it still always sounded cheesy to me. I mean, the interaction occurred in a fast food restaurant line! And yet, it was cute at the same time.

Everywhere in the house, I'm fine, except for the art room. Before Dad died, the garage was where he created art for a short time. However, the art room was the place where we spent the most time together over the years, up until then. Whether it was drawing, painting, talking, we even used to play games in there when I was younger. I don't want to go in the room yet, because then it will feel like he really is gone.

When I get home from school, I glance at the empty spot where Dad's recliner used to be. The chair was already falling apart anyway. The part where you prop your feet on wasn't pulling up all the way. We both know the real reason Mom wanted to get rid of it, though—because it was Dad's recliner.

I pass by Mom's bedroom on the way to my room. It took me about a week to set foot in her room, and even now, some days I imagine he's in the art room working on something or asleep in their bedroom. I wish he was.

When I reach my room, I toss my backpack on the bed and throw on a green dress with thin white stripes and slip on a pair of black flats. I look at myself in the full-size mirror beside my door. Should I even wear a dress? Jessie is always wearing jeans when she goes to work.

I head to the bed and unzip the pocket on the front of my backpack to find my phone, locating Mom's name on it to call her.

"May?" she answers. Mom returned to work as soon as we came back to the house and has been thanking the heavenly stars she has a job. She's only been an accountant for the past year. Mom had started school to earn her degree in accounting, then quit after she had me, staying home until she decided to finish a few years ago.

My dad's life insurance didn't kick in because his death was suicide—that caused a lot of tears from Mom. She couldn't have the funeral she had wanted for Dad, but she made it work.

"Hey, Mom. I'm not sure what to wear for the interview." Walking back to the mirror, I look down at the dress that falls right at my knees.

She lets out a small sigh. "Is this why you're calling me here at work? I told you not to worry about a job right now."

I need this to help save for college, and I don't want it all to fall on Mom's shoulders. Mom said I didn't have to go to work yet, but I told her it would help me feel better by getting out of the house. I *want* to keep myself busy.

"Well, I *would* text you," I say. "You claim you don't know how to text, yet you know how to use a computer?"

She laughs. "Okay, maybe I could text if I wanted to, but it's so impersonal. There are also stories of texts being saved. No one can save anything if I talk over the phone. Not that I'm worried about you saving anything."

I smile. "Untrue. I'm secretly recording you right now."

"We both know that isn't true," she snorts. "Let's figure this out quickly. I may be late coming home tonight, so you might have to make yourself dinner." By making dinner, that's code for me popping a meal into the microwave.

Relaxing on the bed, I cross my ankles. "I already put on the dress, but everyone who works there wears jeans."

"Easy—the dress. If everyone there is wearing jeans, who cares? It's better to shine, my little star, than not."

"Did you just make that up or heard it from somewhere?"

I tease.

"Whatever, it works. Love you."

"Love you, too, Mom. Bye."

Leaving on the dress, I stand up to locate my keys, and they aren't beside me. It never fails me, I'm always misplacing them somehow. I pat along the bed where my backpack is laying. Nothing. I dive under my bed and spot them. "Yes!" I'm not sure how they got under there, but they did. Latching onto the keys, I pull back and manage to hit my head. "No!" I grunt and then rub the sore spot.

Finding my purse, I lock up and book it for the car. I got my license the day I turned seventeen a week ago, and Mom gave me the keys to her car. I would've taken Dad's, but she wanted to drive his car.

The drive takes me maybe twenty minutes, and I spot New and Used Books. Could we have come up with a more generic name? It does scream, *this is what we have to sell here*, though.

Walking the two steps, I almost trip. You would think I have on heels today instead of flats.

Jessie has worked at this used bookstore for the past six months, and as she promised, she got me an interview today. She said, "As long as you smile, you have the job." I can put on a false smile since I've been doing that at school after what happened with Dad.

I spot Jessie as soon as I walk through the door, and she *skips* to me. No. Really. She skips to me. She colored her hair from her usual blonde over the weekend, and I like the new hues. It's now a bright orange with a little bit of yellow infused.

Jessie gives me a side hug. "I missed you,"—she looks at

the pretend watch on her wrist, as if she's reading time—"even though I saw you in first period, fourth period, and lunch."

"People can't get enough of me. What can I say?" I shrug and laugh.

Giggling, she shakes her head. "Let me find Violet. She's probably in the back with one of the applicants."

"How many people is she interviewing for the spot?"

"Three. That means you've got this. Be right back." She turns around and leaves while I stand around looking awkward.

I'm not sure I'll have this if the other people are more qualified than me. I have zero work experience.

"You applying for the job?" a deep, male voice says behind me.

Whirling around, I see no one's there except for stacks and stacks of books. I gaze at the desk, and this is the spot where anyone who wants to sell or trade in books brings them.

"Uh, okay," I say to apparently no one.

Then a tall guy pops up from behind the desk, startling me. He places a large stack of books on the counter beside the cash register.

"Sorry, I had to leave you there for a minute." He glances at me and smiles. "Be right back."

He bends down and vanishes, and when he stands again, he's holding another large stack of books. His hair is a dark auburn and shaggy, with loose curls against tan skin—it works on him.

I stare, not sure what to say, and then I remember he asked me a question. "Oh, yeah, I'm here for an interview with Violet." As my gaze meets his, I see his eyes are the color of honey.

"Good luck. Violet's a feisty one."

Not sure what to say about that since I haven't met her yet, so I go with a common reply. "Thanks."

"What's your name?" He bends down again to pick up more books.

"May?" Jessie calls my name from across the store and motions me over.

I turn back to the guy, and he's all smiles. "See you around, May."

I wave and walk to the back of the store where Jessie is waiting for me, lightly tapping her foot against the gray, ceramic floor.

The aisle I follow to reach her is loaded with books, and the store has so many that I don't know how they make money if they are buying and trading books all the time. They must sell a lot.

"Finally," Jessie says.

"Well, you didn't tell me to wait over here. You told me you would be right back," I say with sarcasm.

Jessie huffs, holding up her arm and flapping her hand down. "Same difference."

I arch a brow.

"Anyway, Violet is ready for you. I put in a good word, so *do not* fail me," she slowly says the words do not, and then lets out a laugh.

I don't want to fail. I need this job. Should I show my desperation in the interview by getting down on my knees and clasping my hands together to beg? Wow, I'd seem hopeless and would most likely get kicked out of here, but I'm open to anything right now. Even if it's something I wouldn't normally do.

Following Jessie back to Violet's office, I stop at the entrance. Holy mother of all things that are purple. Purple curtains, purple flowers, purple wall color, purple pens, and purple hair.

The purple hair must belong to Violet, and her decorations match alarmingly with it. Relaxing my eyes back to their normal position, I know good and well they are wide and fully exposed like open windows.

Violet stands up from her purple chair that she was swiveling side to side in. She walks over and extends her hand toward mine, noticing me peering all around. "You must be May Falkner. As you might guess, purple is my favorite color."

Grabbing her hand, I lightly shake it. "No purple eye contacts?" I blurt out.

Immediately, I want to rope those words back into my mouth and sew my lips together with string. Purple string would be the perfect fit.

She lets out a loud laugh. "If only that were possible. I can't put anything in my eyes, even eye drops are quite the challenge."

Her irises are striking, a grayish-blue that shouldn't be replaced with any contact. She appears too young to have her own office—my guess would be she's around eighteen or nineteen.

Violet glances at Jessie, who is standing in the doorway with her arms crossed over her chest. A slight red tint stains her cheeks from trying to hold back a laugh. "You can help

Nico with the books."

Jessie nods and gives me a thumbs up before she leaves. When Violet looks at Jessie one more time, her thumbs up turns into an awkward five finger wave, and Jessie smiles widely as she turns to leave.

"Take a seat," Violet says, picking up a white piece of paper. I sit down in a cloth chair opposite her. "So, I'm going over your application—this will be your first job?"

I study the paper in her hand, showing my lack of experience in anything except going to school. "Yes, this would be my first job, and I need this to help save up money for college."

I don't dare tell her the real reason for needing the job, which is that my mom might not be able to cover college expenses because of what happened to my dad. I don't want to start looking pitiful in the office.

Violet presses her lips firmly together. "You have goals. I like that. So, I see you're in high school. Would you be able to work any day after school that we need you and on weekends? Will going to school affect you working here?"

"Yes ma'am, and I don't have a problem with working after school and on weekends." I nod.

"You don't need to call me ma'am. Honestly, I'm only trying to act professionally here for my parents' sake."

"Oh." I don't know what else to say.

"This is their store, but they have me manage it. Not that I don't have other things to do. I go to college, too, but in their opinion"—she finger quotes in the air—"'Art Degrees' are pointless."

"You like art?" I ask.

Violet slaps her hands against the desk, and it rattles while knocking a few pens over. "Hell yes, I love art!"

This interview has taken an interesting turn because I can talk about art anytime. "I love art, too! That's what I want to go to college for, except I want to teach it," I say with excitement.

She taps her index finger against her forehead. "I have a proposition for you. You can have this job if you fill in as a model this weekend for a drawing I'm working on for an art show for school. My model flaked out at the last minute. Is that blackmail? Who the hell cares? You were going to have the job anyway. I have to interview a couple of others to make it seem 'fair.'" More finger quotes.

I think I like this girl. "You have a deal. What do you need me to do?"

"Just model and sit still while I draw. You're the exact height I need, and it will only be you and my brother. Before you get that look on your face, don't worry, there won't be any nudity. You two are underage, and I don't need to be sent to jail, and I sure don't want to see my brother in that state." She crinkles her nose and makes a disgusted sound as if she wants to throw up just from mentioning it.

It sounds easy enough. "Okay, I'm game."

Violet holds up her hands and claps them together while tilting her mouth to the side in a half smile. "Yes!" She lifts her purple head to the ceiling like she's thanking the worn tiles above us personally.

I'm not sure what to say, but a steady excitement is now pumping through my veins

"I'll need you at my house this Saturday for the drawing at

nine o'clock in the morning, and you can start work here next Monday after school. Make sure you dress comfortably."

"Thank you so much. I need this job."

"Jessie mentioned you're very dependable and those are the kind of workers we need here. There have been too many flakes I've had to let go. Anyway, I'll text you my address for Saturday." She points at my phone number on the application. "This is a cell phone number, right?"

"Yes, it is."

"Great!" Violet runs around the desk, then hauls me into the quickest hug I have ever had. One second she has her arm around me, and the next she's beside me with her arms at her sides. I'm tall for a girl, and she's tiny. It's awkward, but I give her a weird pat on the back for some reason.

Stepping away from me, Violet lifts her hand to her brow like she has drawn sweat. "Sorry about that. I got excited that I found the right person I've been looking for. As you might've guessed, the professional act is hard to keep up with for too long."

Violet walks me to the office door. "Keep an eye out for my text." Suddenly, she turns and dashes toward her desk, picking up the application while I watch her with questioning eyes. I'm not sure what she's doing, but she lifts her phone, and then my cell phone vibrates in my purse. "I wanted to go ahead and text you before I forget. Anyway, see you Saturday."

I leave the office both excited and nervous, not spotting Jessie until I see her sifting through books at the book trade desk. "How did it go?" Her mouth is open like she's waiting to hear she's won the lottery.

The auburn-haired guy pops out from behind the computer. "Yes, how did it go?"

Jessie sighs. "Ignore Nico."

Okay, so this is Nico—the guy Jessie was sent to help. I'll remember that name and face.

I scan Nico before turning my head back to Jessie. "Well, I start next Monday."

Jessie nods knowingly. "I told you you'd get the job."

"Thanks, Jessie. I owe you big time." And I do.

"Buy me a gallon of any flavor ice cream, and I'll call it even. I may even share some of it with you." She rubs her hands together, probably wishing she had the ice cream right now in her hands.

"After school tomorrow, come by the house. Mom recently bought some."

"Does that include me?" Nico leans on the desk with his forearms on top of it, his chin-length hair sways forward, and a hopeful expression spreads across his face.

Before I can say anything else, Jessie speaks up. "Sorry, Nico, girls only." I wouldn't have minded him tagging along. He seems funny.

Nico's face pulls into a pout, and he does look adorable. "Damn."

Pivoting on my heels, I walk backward to the door. "Well, I'll let you guys get back to work. See you tomorrow, Jessie." Then I turn around and leave as they both say bye. Maybe this is the start of something good in my life.

# Chapter Six

The rest of the week I constantly think about going to Violet's on Saturday. This is mainly because Violet had texted me daily reminders the entire week about Saturday. It doesn't bother me at all, though, because her texts have funny ways of sending the reminders. One message even had a picture of a clock with a rabbit next to it saying, "Don't be late for a very important date."

I wake up in the morning at seven o'clock, and she's already texting me at seven-forty.

Violet: Today is the day!

Me: Do I need to bring anything?

Violet: All you need is yourself.

Setting the phone down, I finish getting ready. I'm not nervous in the slightest because Violet seems cool. I decide to pick up some donuts and kolaches on the way because *I* want a kolache, and I might as well share the wealth.

Snatching the bag from the cashier at the drive-thru, I dive right into it as I pull forward to leave. My stomach rumbles from the lack of breakfast this morning, needing to be filled with this awesome delicacy. It's only a kolache, but when I bite into the melted cheese and greasy sausage, my stomach bids a proper hello.

I change the radio station multiple times on the way to Violet's when it starts to rain. The drive only takes me twenty-five minutes when her house slides into view.

The rain has slowed to a drizzle with only a couple of drops patting me on my face when I exit my car.

Violet's house is big—it has one of those cool driveways that you can pull in on one side and follow the curve to exit. No need for backing out when you can drive forward. The house is made of gorgeous brick and stonework, and there are several tall trees in the front yard with bright green leaves and white flowers on swaying branches.

Strolling up to the porch, I see there's a tall, wooden door with a large oval of glass covering half of it. I don't want to lean forward and peer inside all creeper-like, so I ring the doorbell and step back.

As soon as I move, the door swings open, and the first thing I see is auburn hair. My heart speeds up at the sight of Nico. When he answered, my expression must have looked questioning because he says, "So, I see you made it on time to model for Violet's artwork."

"Um, yeah. I'm supposed to do something for Violet with her brother." I search around for Violet, but I don't see her anywhere.

His grin grows wide. "Well, that would be me. Nico Evitts, at your service."

I don't know why this whole situation seems odd to me, but it does. "Oh. I had no idea you were her brother."

Nico yawns, appearing a little on the tired side. He's

wearing a solid white shirt and black mesh shorts that fall to his knees. His hair is messy, but it looks really good on him. I glance to the right, so it doesn't seem like I'm staring.

"Nicolai, what are you doing hovering at the door? Let May in already," Violet shouts from somewhere in the house.

"Nicolai?" I ask.

His eyes drift to the side and then back at me. "For the most part she remembers to call me Nico, but it's usually Nicolai. Everyone else calls me Nico. However, you can call me whatever you want."

I let out a laugh. "Um, I'll call you Nico."

"That's the way I like it." He smiles.

"Seriously, Nicolai, stop standing at the door flirting with May. We have things to do here." Violet pops into view next to Nico and grabs my wrist, practically yanking me through the doorway. My arm brushes against Nico, and he moves over to let me walk through the opening before I ram him completely.

Violet lets go of my arm, and I rub where she grabbed me. "You know, you're quite strong for being so small."

She crosses her arms, and her short purple hair is standing up everywhere. "I'm not that small."

"You really are, sis," Nico chimes in.

"How old are you two anyway?" I glance from Nico to Violet. "You look close in age."

Uncrossing her arms, Violet points at herself and then at Nico. "I'm nineteen and Nico is seventeen. He's a senior in high school."

Nico looks like he's nineteen—but then again, I'm not good at guessing anyone's age. I'm always way off.

"And how old are you?" Nico asks.

I stand up straight. I'm five-foot-nine—a few inches shorter than Nico. "I'm seventeen, too."

Violet pipes in to end our pointless chatter. "Okay, let's get started."

"Here, I also brought some breakfast for you guys, if you're hungry." I hand Nico the bag of donuts and kolaches, and he digs right in, pulling out a kolache and taking a huge bite. I'm still full from mine, but I can't help admiring how good that one looks.

I follow Violet up the stairs, and Nico is right behind me. The house has wood floors throughout, and I hear every creak and squeak as we walk.

On the way up, Nico talks to me about school. I already know Violet attends college, but Nico is a grade ahead of me in twelfth grade. I'm a little disappointed he goes to a different high school because he seems like he would be fun to hang around with at school. Then I remember I'll be seeing him at work, so it kind of makes up for it.

"Holy moly," I blurt, coming to a halt.

Violet's room has even more purple than her office had—the sheets, walls, curtains, dresser drawers, stuffed animals, are all different shades of purple. Somehow with the different shades and the way she has it set up, it looks good.

"You should see my room," Nico says.

I whip around and face him. "Is your room this purple, too?"

He shrugs. "Maybe? You would have to see to find out."

Violet grimaces. "Seriously, Nicolai, grow up."

Nico's expression turns innocent. "Oh, give it a rest,

Violet—you know I didn't mean it like that."

Ignoring Nico, Violet faces me with growing excitement. "Anyway." She walks to the bed, grabs a folded set of clothing, and plops them into my hands. "I need you to change into this. The bathroom is right there." She smiles as she points in the direction of a hallway door that I assume leads to it.

Clasping me by the wrist again, she drags me down the hall while Nico waits in the bedroom. "Let me know if you need anything else." Then she leaves me standing there.

I walk inside with the clothes in hand, and it's larger than my bedroom. If only Dad was here to see this bathroom, I would ask him to redo ours like this—only it would be a smaller version.

The sink is like a bowl sitting on top. Migrating toward it, I turn on the faucet just to watch the water run and then shut it off. *Yes, I definitely need one of these.*

I slide off my clothes, then unfold the shirt and shorts Violet handed me. These must be from Violet's wardrobe because they are incredibly small.

The top is a black camisole with a built-in bra, and I put it on—it stops right below my belly button. Then I slide on the black shorts that barely cover my bottom. Nothing is hanging out, but they're skin tight.

Back in the hallway, I find Violet waiting with a brush in her hand. Turning me around, she starts brushing my hair like a doll.

"You know that I can brush my hair, right?" I say.

She stops mid brush and stares me square in the eye. "Everyone loves getting their hair messed with by someone else." Then she continues brushing. The situation is odd but having someone brush your hair does feel nice at the same time.

"So, what does Nico have to wear?" I doubt he has to wear anything like what I'm wearing.

Violet pulls the brush away from my hair. "Well, he's wearing the white shirt you saw earlier, except he's going to have on white shorts."

"Like mine?" I laugh.

"No, no. Like regular white shorts that come to the knee. We are going for an angel and demon vibe."

I nod. "I'm the demon, right?"

"Yes, and Nico is going to be our little angel. This is the one time in his life, he will be." She sounds amused.

I follow her back into her purple inspired room where Nico is already sitting on the floor in front of the bed. "It's about time," he says with a grin.

Violet grunts. "Oh, please. What else do you have going on today?"

Staring in my direction, Nico seems to study what I'm wearing. It's way more than a bathing suit, but I haven't gone swimming since I was younger. "Maybe I'm going to be hanging out with May?"

My heart quickens, so I pat away invisible dust on my shirt, avoiding looking at his face.

"Yeah, you're going to be hanging out with May for this drawing. Now, park it in the way I told you to sit earlier," Violet instructs.

"You could at least say please." Nico bats his eyelashes in her direction—Violet ignores him. He then props his back against the footboard of the bed and straightens his legs out.

His T-shirt is tight against his arms and chest—the shorts are mesh and right above his knees like the ones he was wearing earlier, except these are white.

Violet focuses on me now. "Okay, as I told you earlier, we are going for this modern-day angel/demon vibe. I'll be drawing in the wings, horns and all that jazz later."

My eyes slide from left to right, waiting for her to continue. She must have already explained this to Nico.

"You are going to go sit in Nico's lap with your knees on either side of his legs. Your arms are going to wrap around to his back, and your face will be leaning against his shoulder facing his neck."

Okay, this is going to be a big pile of awkward. When Violet asked me to pose with her brother, I don't know what I assumed exactly. Maybe that we would be posed sitting next to each other, not me on top of him. The last time I was even sort of close to a guy was in eighth grade. I had a crush on this guy Bryan, and Jessie told him I liked him. She'd then told me he'd asked for me to meet him before school in the back of the building. I met him behind the school, and he kissed me—with tongue. I was excited until he wanted me to come to his house after school to do more than that.

I was fourteen, and I told him I only wanted to kiss for now. He ignored me after that.

That was my first and only kiss. I've had a couple of guys at school ask me to hang out when I started high school, but I wasn't that interested in them.

Oh, well. It can't be that weird. Real models do racier poses with people they don't know all the time.

My palms moisten from nervousness as I walk to Nico.

"Stop right there," Violet says with seriousness. "Make sure you don't sit directly on his birthday package. You know how guys get."

A belly curdling laugh escapes me, and I glance at Nico, his eyes wide, looking like he wants to run out of the room, but then he smiles. "Whatever, sis, I do have some control." That loosens my nervousness.

When I get into position, I sit a little higher on Nico, wrapping my arms around him and placing my face like Violet instructed me to do. My forehead and the bridge of my nose are resting against Nico's warm, smooth skin, and he smells pleasant—like he just took a shower this morning.

I don't want to breathe in too deeply and seem weird for smelling him. So, to avoid being strange, I keep my breathing normal, but I can't control the rapid beats of my heart.

"Okay, do you remember what I told you to do, Nico?" Violet is tapping a pencil against her palm.

"Mmhmm." One of his hands wraps around my upper back, and the other hand is on my neck, clasping some of my hair in his fist. I like how it feels.

"Okay, sit still. I'm going to take a picture first for backup in case I need to correct anything." I can't see her, but I hear her snapping different photographs with her phone while she moves around us. The pictures stop, and Violet walks away to start drawing.

As we sit here, the only sounds I hear are the back-and-forth strokes of Violet's pencil against the paper, and Nico's soft, continuous breaths. I wonder what he's feeling at this moment.

His chest moves slowly back and forth, and my heart has

slowed down. Sitting with him feels comfortable, even though I don't know Nico.

This must be why people who model love their job—at the moment everything seems real. Even though you don't always know who you're working with, you can be someone else and pretend as if you're in a whole different reality, until real life comes crashing back.

After sitting for such a long time, my legs are beginning to cramp, but then Violet slams her pencil against the desk and sighs happily. "All done!"

I don't want to let go, but I do. "I think my legs are asleep," I say.

"Your legs?" Nico laughs. "My legs are!"

I move to swing my leg over his hip, and he holds me by the waist as he helps me off his lap. My legs are restless, and I continuously straighten and bend them, while Nico rises off the floor to shake his legs out.

As I walk toward Violet to see the artwork, she immediately covers it with her lips puckered out. "No one can see it until it's completed."

All right then. I slowly back away, hoping not to disturb her masterpiece further.

"Don't worry. You aren't the only one who can't see it until it's finished." Nico shrugs.

Violet turns away from her work and sets her pencil down, tapping her fingers together. "Nothing personal, but I don't want anyone having an unfinished image in their brain."

That makes sense to me, so I head to the bathroom to change back into my clothes. When I come out, Nico is waiting at the end of the hall, and Violet's door is shut.

Nico shuffles toward me and points at the closed door. "She has to finish her art with no interruptions," he groans.

I get it. All artists have their own way of doing things. I shrug and say, "I can do art almost anywhere—it just depends on the person."

"So, then you aren't as extreme as Violet?" Nico chuckles.

"No, I'm more on the technical side of things. I love to do art all the time, whether it's painting or drawing, but I would rather teach it and help others perfect their natural skills."

He stops right before we start down the stairs. "Yeah? I want to teach, too, but I want to teach music."

Grabbing the rail, I walk down the stairs. "What do you play?"

"Everything."

"No, really. What instrument?"

Tilting his head to the side, he grins. "I have a knack for being able to pick up any instrument and play well, but guitar is my favorite."

Searching through my purse, I locate my keys. "Maybe I can listen to you play sometime? I like music, but I can't play at all." I think it would be fun to hear him play.

We're already at the doorway, and he reaches for the handle, giving me a crooked grin. "Maybe."

Stepping out onto the porch, I say, "When Violet comes out of her room, tell her I said 'bye' and that I'll be at work on Monday."

"I'll let her know, and see you on Monday. I'm the one who'll be training you."

"Sounds good." I fidget with my keys, liking the idea of him being the one to train me.

Nico runs a hand through his hair as if he wants to ask me something else, but he doesn't.

Waving bye to him, I stroll back to my car. Before, I was feeling nervous about my first day of work, but not so much anymore.

# Chapter Seven

After I left Nico and Violet's place, the rest of the weekend I stayed at home with my mom. The entire portion was spent trying to comfort her while she cried more about my dad. We have had our ups and downs, and I get that we all have different emotions, but I want her to move forward the way that I am. I would sit across from her at the dinner table, letting her know that I was still here for her, but she'd just say it isn't the same without him. It did hurt my feelings, but she has to want to help herself, too.

Snatching my phone off the couch, I call my mom before leaving for my first day of work. "Hey, Mom, don't forget I'm going to be home late tonight."

"Okay, sweetie, have a great first day at your new job. Remember if you end up not liking it, you can quit."

I know that's what she wants me to do, but I know the job will help. "Alright, Mom. I better let you go since you're working. Love you."

"Love you, too." I can practically feel her smile over the phone.

Her mood is good today. These are the days where she does a one-eighty and sounds okay. I know people handle things differently, but I want my mom to be like she was.

I still get sad, but I've been able to go days without crying at night now. After my dad died, I would fall asleep with tears in my eyes and wake up the next morning feeling panic flutter inside my chest.

Today, I woke up, and I was okay. Jessie has been a great friend—she's been there for me when I needed someone to talk to, and if I didn't have her, I don't know what I would do. I won't be seeing her at work today, as she has the day off.

Leaving my house, I head for the bookstore and arrive a little early. I sit in my car for a few minutes before I walk inside, prepping myself for this new experience.

I thought I wasn't going to be nervous, but the nerves hit me as soon as I pass through the door. I'm not sure exactly where I'm supposed to go, or what I'm supposed to do. Violet must be a mind reader because she sprouts up out of nowhere beside me. "There's the new girl. I've been watching the minutes tick by on my clock waiting for you to arrive."

"Really?" I sound surprised.

"No." Violet laughs. "I saw you parking your car when I walked by, and you seemed all nervous and stuff. I decided to give you the honor of pulling yourself together, so you didn't look like an idiot."

Too late, I already feel like a complete idiot.

She paces to the back of the store. "Follow me, and I'll show you where to clock in." She stops and glances back at me. "By the way, I forgot to thank you for helping me out on Saturday. The drawing would've turned out terrible if it had only been Nico."

I'm not too sure about that. I think Nico could pull off any picture. "No problem. I had fun."

She gives me a wink. "I bet you did."

Is she insinuating I like Nico? I don't even know anything about him besides him being really cute and, apparently, can play a ton of instruments. And I have to see that to believe it.

Violet shows me where to clock in and hands me my card. After swiping the card, I place it back in the slot that reads my name.

She turns and leads me through an aisle of books until we reach the sell and trade books counter. "This is where you'll be working."

Nico happens to round the corner with a gigantic box of books in his hands, his face red from the strain.

Violet leans her head forward. "No need to break your back, little brother. You could've carried a few books at a time."

He shoots Violet a dirty look while setting the box of books at the sell and trade desk. "You're the one who told me to quit slacking and bring the box in as quickly as possible."

"I did say that, didn't I?" She presses her index finger against her chin, shrugs, and turns to walk away. "Anyway, focus on getting May trained. Her success at her job depends on you relaying your skills and knowledge to her."

That last sentence should have me a little worried, but I like Violet already.

"Hey, newbie, are you ready to learn the trade skills over here?" I turn to Nico who is tapping the edge of the desk with his foot.

I hold up my hands in surrender. "I'm all yours."

"I like that answer. Now get over here," he says with a

smile, causing a small extra thump in my chest. It's going to be hard to not find him adorable.

Nico shows me the basic aspects of how to perform the job. People bring in books, and I search through the computer to see how many we have in the store, then I compare them with used prices elsewhere. When people bring them in to sell or trade, all the books must be organized and separated.

Violet decides whether she wants books for sale in the store or through the website. There's another bin by the desk for donations. She or Nico usually bring them up to the hospital for patients to get first dibs who want them, and any remaining books go to the library.

The shift has been easy and flown by. I think it's because Nico has been able to keep me entertained. When he sorts through the books, he hums softly to himself, sometimes strumming his fingers along the desk or the books as he lightly taps his foot against the floor.

If I didn't already know he was a musician, I would now know just by watching him and how he's an instrument himself.

Nico shifts his gaze to the clock hanging on the wall. "Break time!"

I close the cover of a book. "Oh, okay. Go ahead."

"You and me, candy store, next door," he says it as if I know what he's talking about.

"What are you rambling on about?" I glance around.

"The. Candy. Store. Next. Door." He draws each word out slowly.

Walking around the counter, I peer out the side window and see a huge sign that reads: Pete's Candy and More.

"There's a candy store next door!" I say excitedly. Then I stop and cock my head. "Wait, this is an actual candy store, right, and not some weird innuendo? I know how some of those stores work."

Giving me a sly look, he whispers, "Then we'll go next door and find out now, won't we?"

"Go ahead. I don't want to leave the area unattended." I don't want to seem like I'm slacking off on my first day.

He kicks my foot lightly with his. "Do you know how pissed Violet would be if I left you by yourself to cover the desk on your first day?"

I shake my head and smile.

He makes the slit-throat motion with his thumbnail gliding across his throat. "I would be dead."

Picking up the phone on the desk, Nico clicks the button to Violet's office line. "Violet, we're going to go on break now. Can you keep a lookout over here?" His eyebrows scrunch down. "Are you really that busy? I bet you a hundred dollars you're drawing a picture in there. You are, aren't you? I knew it!"

Shaking his head, he taps his fingers against his leg. "Yeah, we're going next door to Pete's. May didn't know the place existed."

Pulling the phone away from his ear, he stares at it and shakes his head before hanging up.

I glance up, and Violet is headed our way. "You haven't been to the candy store? What world are you living in?"

"The same one as you?" I guess.

Violet's hands pound against the counter. "No, you aren't! Go, now!"

I'm seriously interested in finding out more about this candy store and seeing what all the fuss is about.

Nico is already pulling me to the door. "And bring me something back!" Violet calls.

Outside, Nico and I walk side by side through the parking lot. The gravel underneath our shoes makes crunching sounds, and the heat penetrates my skin.

Nico elbows me in the arm. "So, you've really never noticed this place?"

"No!" I laugh. "Out of all the months that Jessie has worked here, I've never been here. When I interviewed, that was the first time I had been to the bookstore. As you will come to realize one day, I don't pay as much attention to my surroundings as I should." I hold up my finger. "And seriously, I would've assumed it was a lingerie store. I mean, there aren't any dessert decorations on the sign or the building anywhere." I let my eyes roam across the building and then back at the big sign.

We approach the store and come to a stop at the door. "There's a cupcake right here on the door." He taps the picture of the pink-frosted cupcake on the glass with his index finger.

"Oh, okay. One small, tiny cupcake, that I would never have seen without you graciously pointing it out. And, thank you for that." The small, pink cupcake is maybe the size of my fist.

He opens the door, still beaming with pleasure for pointing out the cupcake. "After you."

"Such a gentleman."

I gaze around, astonished. This is the best candy store I've ever seen in my life. There are all types of candy along the walls. The white chocolate section is calling my name, and I walk toward it.

Staring side to side as I head over to study the treats, I notice an ice cream section, cupcakes, smoothies, and any dessert you can think of.

Nico is right beside me when I look to my left. "When you said candy store, I was thinking of a rundown gas station with pre-packaged candy. This place is freaking amazing."

"I'm thinking about saying I told you so." Nico bumps his arm with mine.

"Don't even think about it," I warn. His smile grows wider, and I stare a moment too long at his mouth before focusing back on the candy.

He plucks a white bag from a silver hook on the wall. "This place is pretty much the hangout spot after school or on the weekends."

What do the kids at our school usually do? I always hear them talking about movies. "I think the kids at our school mainly go to the movies or the mall. I don't do a lot."

Or at least over the past couple of years, I haven't. I usually hang around my house—most of the time Jessie comes over, or I go to her house.

Watching my dad deteriorate and seeing Mom cry all the time had me not wanting to do much besides my homework or art.

Nico hands me one of the white bags from the wall. "Choose your poison."

When I grab the bag from his hand, it makes a crinkling sound. "My poison is anything right here on this wall." Lifting my hand up, I point at all the white chocolate candies, and then tap rapidly at a glass box filled with white chocolate pretzels. I turn my head to the right, and my eyes strike gold when I see the white chocolate balls. The small paper sign reads that they're filled with creamy, white chocolate.

"No way. Brown chocolate all the way." Nico wrinkles his nose in disgust before filling up his bag with chocolate pretzels and other brown chocolate assortments.

Lifting the red lid, I grab the scoop and fill half my bag up with the white chocolate balls. Then I move to the white chocolate squares with peanut butter inside that are displayed directly next to the white chocolate balls.

Closing the lid, I set the scoop down and walk toward Nico. "What are you going to get for Violet?" I ask as Nico folds the top of his bag down.

His head turns to the cupcake section, and a small frown appears on his face. "Geez, thanks for reminding me. I almost forgot about her, and I would never have heard the end of it. I mean, seriously! Would. Have. Never. Heard. The. End."

I don't normally giggle, but I let out a loud giggle that echoes. I'm aware it probably sounds stupid, but the way he said that is the best thing I've seen in a while—with his finger moving back and forth with each word.

"Are you crying?" He laughs.

"Just give me a minute." I can't stop laughing. "Hold this." Handing him my bag of chocolate, I wipe the tears away from my eyes. "I'm good now."

"Are you sure? We can do this whole scene over again." He hands back my bag, and I head toward the counter.

"Let's not." I grin.

"Do you want anything else?" He places his bag on the

counter.

"No, this will hold me over," I say. But it will only hold me over for the day because I'm going to finish the whole bag. I won't be able to control myself.

He yanks the candy out of my hand and passes it to a middle-aged woman who's reading a book on a stool.

I stare at him. "You know I can pay for that."

"Can I also have a key lime pie cupcake," he asks the lady before turning back to me. "I'm sure you can, but I got you today."

I'm not going to argue back about that. "Thank you."

"You're welcome."

A small breeze has started to blow as we leave the store. The wind ruffles Nico's hair all around, and I want to move it out of his face. I'm beginning to find him more than cute, especially with his funny personality. I think if I keep working here with him, it's going to be hard not to fall for him. To ignore that thought, I plop a white chocolate ball in my mouth, and it's pure heaven as it melts in my mouth.

I take one step in the door, and Violet slides out from behind the desk. "Where's my cupcake?"

"Sorry, sis. They were fresh out of cupcakes today."

Violet's face falls. "What?"

I roll my eyes. "He's kidding."

Nico hands her the cupcake bag, and she smacks his arm. "You don't have to be an ass. You know how I get about my cupcakes." Then she walks off.

The rest of the night is slow, and Nico and I talk about movies back and forth. We settle on eventually making each other watch the ones the other hasn't seen. I have first pick since we battled it out with rock-paper-scissors and I won.

I get off work before he does. "Goodnight," I say and grab my things to leave.

"See you tomorrow, May."

I smile as I walk to my car. Then I stop, feeling guilty for smiling and being happy after what happened with my dad.

# Chapter Eight

The past three months have gotten better for me because of working at the bookstore. Meeting Violet and Nico has been the perfect distraction from everything. Violet is hilarious in her subtle way, and Nico is something special. My feelings have grown into something for him, and I want so much to let him know. I'm scared that he may not feel the same way. Sometimes I think he's flirting, but then I don't know if that's just how he is.

"What time am I picking you up tomorrow night for the art exhibit?" Nico asks. He has his arms sprawled across the countertop, and he gives me an expecting expression while cocking his head.

I close the book I'm trying to find a price for and look up at Nico's smiling face. "What are you talking about?"

"Didn't Violet tell you?" He runs a finger along the edge of the counter. "She said she told you already. She did let me know right before work, even though she has known about it for quite some time."

Violet walks by at that very moment and stops in front of the desk, narrowing her eyes slightly. "I did tell you guys a couple of weeks ago."

Pushing away from the desk, I place my hands on my hips. "No, you didn't. I would've remembered that."

"Yeah, Violet. At least one of us would've remembered," Nico pipes in.

Violet shrugs. "Maybe I said it to you guys in my head and thought I had told you two. Anyway, it's tomorrow night at seven." Then she walks away.

"Your sister can be very odd, Nico." She's different, but for the whole three months I've been here, I have come to enjoy our conversations.

He nods in agreement. "You try living seventeen years with her." Nico stands up and leans his hip against the counter. "Back to what I was asking, what time do you want me to pick you up?"

I laugh. "I might give you a time if you tell me what this is."

Scuffing his feet around the desk, he lifts a stack of books off the floor and sorts through them. "It's some student art exhibit her class is doing, and each student is going to have a few of their pieces on display." He gestures at me and then back at himself. "Our picture is going to be one of the pieces hanging up for everyone to see. Prepare to become an instant celebrity."

I shake my head, fighting a smile. "Right, we'll have to start avoiding all the paparazzi."

"Exactly. If I had my sunglasses in here right now, I'd put them on." Nico points at his eyes and grins.

Laughing, I finish going through the last book in my stack and call Juan Mendoza over the intercom to come and get his estimate on the books. The intercom gives off a crackling sound that Violet has asked her parents to fix, but it has made the noise ever since I've been here. Juan walks up, takes the cash, and strolls away.

Nico finishes his stack of books and calls Jenny Martin to the desk. This time the intercom gives off a little less of a crackle and mutes the end of Jenny's last name. Jenny saunters up with a pile of books in her hands and takes the money Nico hands her. She then walks to the cashier to purchase way more books than she brought in.

I turn back to Nico. "Have you seen the finished drawing, yet? I haven't thought to ask Violet about it."

That's a lie. I haven't forgotten to ask Violet about the drawing. I've been anxious to see it, but then I changed my mind, not wanting more memories of that day with Nico to surface than they already do.

For the past three months, work has been my haven. I come here and forget about what has been going on at home with my mom and her mood swings. It's like that part of my brain shuts completely off when I'm at work.

Nico rubs his palm against the back of his neck. "You know, I've been bugging her continuously to show me, but she keeps saying her art is top secret. Back to the point of my first question, what time?"

I huff as if the question is getting on my nerves when in fact I'm excited. "You sure you don't want me to meet you there?"

"What? And give up finding out where you live, so I can drive by your house all the time?" He pauses. "In case you really think I may have stalker potential, that's a joke."

Leaning my back against the desk, I cross my arms over

my chest. "I don't know, Nico. Sometimes you do give me that vibe," I joke. "I guess you could pick me up at six?"

"What? Is this a date?" Jessie walks by with a cart of books, catching the last sentence I said.

"No," we say at the same time.

"Oh." Jessie looks intrigued. "Where are we going, then?"

I tell her about the art exhibit that Violet is going to be a part of, and how the drawing she did of us is going to be displayed there.

Turning to Nico, she drops her hands from the cart. "Can you swing by to pick me up after you pick up May?"

I don't know why I feel disappointed by her question, but I do. It isn't as if he's my boyfriend, but it would've been nice to go with just Nico.

He shrugs. "Sure. Just let me know where you guys live."

Damn. Oh, well. Jessie can talk to me if Nico goes MIA chatting to other people, since I won't know anyone else there besides Violet, and she'll most likely be occupied showing off her art. I hate going to places if I don't have someone to talk to because I'm not great at striking up conversations with strangers.

The rest of the shift breezes by, and Nico gets off at the same time I do. His car is parked next to mine, and I'm about to sit in my driver seat when he pulls me back by my purse strap. "Oh, I forgot to ask you for your number—in case I get lost or something."

Why do I feel like bouncing up and down? *Cool it, May. You can be such a loser sometimes.* "Sure." I tell him my number while trying to hide my enthusiastic smile.

"Great. I sent you a text, so you have mine, too." My phone

beeps at that exact moment.

Telling him thanks and to have a good night, I immediately get in my car. Before I leave, I dig through my bag to find the phone, adding his number to my contacts and thinking about what a freaking nerd I am.

♥

When I get home from work, Mom is sitting on the couch already changed into her pajamas. Let's see what kind of mood she's in today.

I don't want to be insensitive, but sometimes she seems okay, and other times it's the complete end of the world. I get it, I do. I have my days, too, but I understand and am ready for her to progressively get better.

I want to remember the good times with Dad, like when he would take me fishing. Most of the time, I didn't even catch anything, but it was fun because it was something Dad and I got to do alone.

After I set my purse down, I look to find Mom already walking to the kitchen. "Hey, sweetie. Do you want me to make you something to eat?"

This would be one of her better days, then. "No, but thanks, Mom. I ate a sandwich at work on my lunch break, so I'm just going to grab a snack and get ready for bed."

"Are you sure? In case you have a lot of homework, I did all your laundry and hung it up already so you don't have to worry about it." She moves to sit down on the couch and resumes her comfortable position.

Hiding my cringe, I say, "Thanks." I prefer to do my

laundry. When she goes to hang all my stuff up, she never puts anything in the right spot—then I can't find what I need.

I eat a yogurt and then get ready for bed, falling asleep to Mom crying again, and I don't know how to make her better.

♥

The next day at school flies by quickly. At lunch, Jessie talks excitedly about the art show, and she's more eager about the cute, college guys that may be there.

Jessie turned eighteen two months ago. Technically, she's supposed to be a senior, but she was held back in kindergarten by her mom, who thought she needed to mature a little bit. As soon as she hit eighteen, she began complaining about all the high school boys and how immature they are.

I told her maybe she should stop trying to date the immature ones, because the guys she picks, you can tell instantly from looking at them they're no good. I have tried to give her tips, but she's going to do what she wants. Not that I have any real experience to hand out.

When I get home from school, Mom is already there. "Short day today at work?" I ask.

She relaxes on a bar stool at the counter, sipping a cup of coffee. "Yes. The boss got some news that he's getting child support from his ex-wife. You don't hear a lot about the man getting child support, so he decided to let us all leave early with a full day's pay."

Setting my backpack on the floor by the door, I take a seat on the barstool next to hers. "Wow. That's pretty awesome."

After taking another sip of her coffee, she sets it down and says, "I asked the boss if I could take off next week. I know it's short notice, but I'm going to be flying out on Sunday and coming back the following Sunday."

I smack my fingers against the counter. "Flying out? Where?" I don't want to fly out anywhere. I have work and school.

"Your Uncle Jim called. He's having trouble dealing with losing his brother. You know he's all alone."

"Why doesn't he fly out here instead?"

"I don't know, sweetie. He's older than your dad was and doesn't have the money." He's ten years older than my dad was. It took my grandparents a long time before they were able to have another child.

"Do you want me to go with you?" I don't want to, but I will if she makes me.

She shakes her head. "No. I don't want you to have to miss a whole week of school."

I don't mind staying by myself, since most of my days are going to be spent at work or school. "Tell Uncle Jim I said hello."

Mom shoots me a stern look. "You won't be staying by yourself—you'll be staying with Mrs. Jenkins."

I groan. "Come on, Mom. You know I love Mrs. Jenkins, but I can't stay the night there. Her house has an old lady smell, and she only has one bed—the odor will stay with me when I leave if I sleep there."

Mom gives me a grin. "She offered to let you sleep in her bed while she takes the couch."

I tug at the end of my shirt and then release it. "Please, Mom. I'm seventeen, that's practically an adult. Most of my days will be at work and school anyway, so I could just stay here. If I need anything I can go next door," I beg. "I can even go over there and check in with her."

Mom chews on the side of her bottom lip. "I don't know."

"Please." Her 'I don't know' usually means yes if I say please a second time.

"Okay, I will let Mrs. Jenkins know. You better not let me down, May. And you're a hundred percent sure you're okay with me leaving for a week?" She tilts her head down with her eyes boring straight into mine, like she'll know if anything happens.

"I won't. And yes, I'll be okay. Plus, Mrs. Jenkins is right next door if I change my mind." After that's settled, I head to my room and am practically leaping for joy that I can sleep in my bed.

The first thing I do is walk straight to the closet and search for what to wear tonight, but I don't want to get overdressed either. It isn't like I'm going to some big gala or anything. I decide to go with my jeans I already have on, but I put on a nicer shirt.

My phone beeps at five-thirty.

Nico: Hey. I'm headed your way.

Me: Okay.

Nico: See you soon.

I smile to myself and decide to put some makeup on. Right when I finish getting ready, the doorbell rings. I grab my purse and hurry for the door.

"Oh. You're going out?" Ugh. I forgot to ask Mom if I could go.

Slowly, I pivot back to Mom with one foot still facing the door ready to jet. "Yes, Mom. I'm going to an art exhibit displaying sketches that a girl from work drew. Remember the one I posed for?"

"Okay, tell Jessie to come in. I haven't seen her in a while." Mom sets down the TV remote beside her.

It hasn't been that long since she has seen Jessie. Mom saw her on Tuesday when she came over to work on her homework with me. "Jessie isn't here. We're going to pick her up right now."

Mom's eyes widen. "Oh?"

"He's a friend from work—his name's Nico. He was part of the art project that his sister drew." Please don't ask any more questions.

The bell rings again, and Mom's eyebrows raise. "You didn't tell me you posed for a picture with a boy? You aren't going anywhere until I meet him."

I roll my eyes. "It wasn't a nude picture." And she didn't ask if there was going to be anyone else posing for the drawing.

She mumbles something as I walk and open the door. Nico is standing outside like he's lost or something. "I thought maybe you weren't here."

"My car is right there." I point. "So, I can't leave until my mom meets you. Can you come in for a second? She doesn't want me to leave with a 'stranger' tonight."

He rubs his hands together. "I *love* meeting people's parents."

# Chapter Nine

*Nico* steps in, and I close the door behind him, leading the way to where Mom is sitting. She's lost her relaxed pose, and her lips are pursed, attempting to look stern. Underneath, I can see she's hiding how happy she is about me bringing a boy over. "Mom, this is Nico. Nico, this is my mom."

As soon as Nico smiles and starts chatting with my mom, she acts like she has known him forever.

When I started high school, Mom was asking me about boyfriends. When was I going to go out on my first date? When was I going to homecoming? When was I going to invite a boy over? Now, it's like all those questions have been answered.

Mom asks Nico questions about school and work, and I know she'll keep doing it unless I interrupt. "Mom, we need to leave if we're going to make it on time. We're picking up Jessie."

Mom appears a little crestfallen about us leaving so soon, but walks us to the door. "Don't worry, but make sure you're home by twelve. Have fun."

Twelve? My curfew is usually eleven. I don't think the art show will last that late since it starts at seven.

Nico opens the car door for me, and my eyes scan him over. He's looking more adorable than usual in a pair of jeans, a plaid button-up shirt with the sleeves rolled up, and a pair of Converse. "Such a gentleman."

"I would say my mom raised me right, but it was Violet. Growing up, she went through a diva stage," he says, giving me a huge grin as he shuts the door. I can totally see a young diva Violet.

He gets in the car and starts the engine. "Where's your dad? I wouldn't have minded meeting him, too."

I stiffen. Out of all our conversations, I haven't talked about my parents. It never came up, and Jessie didn't say anything about it around work either.

"Oh, um, my dad passed away in August." Focusing on my hands, I can't bring myself to see the sympathy on his face.

"I'm sorry, May—I had no idea. Do you want to talk about it?"

I finally glance up at him—his eyes do have sympathy, but his expression is saying if I need him, he'll listen.

Reluctantly, I drag my gaze away from his. "Not right now, but maybe one day." And I mean it. I will discuss it with him, but not today. I want tonight to be fun.

He nods. "Don't hesitate if you want to talk about it, alright?"

"Alright."

My phone beeps and I pull it out of my purse to check it.

Jessie: Did you forget about me?

Me: No. Mom had an interview with Nico.

Jessie: Ugh. Parents.

Me: See you shortly.

Setting the phone down, I look at Nico. "Jessie thought we forgot about her." Honestly, I kind of did. Nico is the first boy who has ever come around the house. Over the years, I haven't had a lot of guy friends either.

"Talk about impatient." Nico laughs. "We're still going to arrive early."

She is impatient. All. The. Time. She's always dependable, though. Anytime I've needed her for anything—whether it was Dad, homework, helping me get my job—she's right here.

As soon as we pull up in front of Jessie's house, neither one of us gets out of the car because she's already flying out the door toward us.

"Finally," she says, breathing heavily. Jessie sits in the back seat and attempts to buckle her seatbelt three times when it finally clicks. "I was going out of my mind listening to the twins bicker back and forth over a video game!"

Jessie's twin brothers are in eighth grade. One day she loves them, and then the next, she wants to ship them off to another planet.

She chatters the whole way. Nico and I exchange glances because Jessie will start asking questions, but then she'll answer them herself. It's quite entertaining.

"Nico, how many students are having their art displayed?" Before he has an opportunity to reply, she answers for him. "I bet there will be a lot."

"May, what kind of art is there going to be?" I crane my neck around the seat to take a guess. "Oh, I bet there will be all kinds of stuff. Ceramic, paint, charcoal. What else is there, May? You're an artist, too."

Laughing, I settle back in my seat because she starts again.

Nico turns into the school for the art show, and the parking lot is already filled with cars.

Once inside the building, there are people standing in every available space of the room, studying canvases lined up against the wall in front of us. At both ends of the wall, there's a hall on each side. Jessie walks forward and gazes at a section that has stained glass—the colors are vivid and beautiful.

Strolling with Nico down the hall on the left, I spot a section displaying watercolor paintings. Watercolor is my favorite, maybe because it was the first kind of paint I remember Dad teaching me. Most kids begin with watercolor and then leave it behind as they grow and find a new hobby. Me? I could bask in it for an eternity.

Violet pops up in front of us, pulling me out of the moment. "Are you guys going to stand here all day? Come see mine, and then you can look at everyone else's."

Waving us to follow her, she then turns and walks off— her purple head drifts away as she leaves us in the dust. "Sure, sis, lead the way," Nico calls.

We follow her farther down the hall toward the end, until she stops in front of a canvas of an old tree that she has sketched. It's twisted and remarkable. There's a fairy tale vibe coming from her sketch—someone in a cloak is peering from behind the gnarled tree, but you can't quite make out the expression.

She points to another one that has a girl with a boa constrictor wrapped around her shoulders. The snake is staring directly at the person viewing the sketch, while the girl is gazing off in another direction so you can only see the side of her face.

The hand holding the snake is covered in bangles all the way down her arm. By seeing the snake's face in this picture, it's as if the reptile has all the control.

Last, Violet points to the canvas of Nico and me. I'm impressed and forget for a moment it's of us. I've seen loads of angel and demon artwork, but the emotions the drawing has me feeling—are good.

Long horns take root at the top of my head, and sharp claws sprout from my fingertips. The demon is terrifying, but the expression on the face is human—*my face*.

Violet drew beautiful wings on Nico that are amazing, and I want to reach into the picture and brush my hand across one of those feathered edges to feel their texture.

Turning to Nico, I tug on his arm. "You look just like an angel."

"You look just like a demon." He grins, and pokes me on my side, right below my rib.

"Are you scared?" I taunt, and I poke him back.

He gives me a daring grin. "Only if you want me to be."

"I'll get back to you on that," I snicker. I want to tell Nico he can be anything he wants for me, but I hold that in.

Instead, I tell Nico I need to find a restroom, and I leave him standing with Violet. It takes me a few minutes to locate it, since I had to walk all the way back to the front and take the other hall.

When I come out of the restroom, Jessie yanks me to the side. "Don't tell me you're stalking me at the bathroom now.

Creeping isn't appealing," I joke.

"I was looking all over for you, and then Violet told me you had gone to the bathroom." Jessie's eyes are wide, and she's more fidgety than usual.

"Did you find your dream college guy, yet?" I dig through my purse to find a mint and reach out to hand her one, but she shakes it off.

She lets out a sigh. "No. He must go to a different college. I'll find him one day." She shakes her head. "Stop trying to distract me."

I place the pack of mints back in my purse. "What are you talking about, Jess?"

She crinkles her nose. "I know you're into Nico. I know that look, except any other time you have been into a guy, it was never this intense."

I pause for a minute, then arch a brow. "Intense, huh?" I'm surprised she didn't ask me about this sooner. Jessie is more of the one who will talk about a guy she likes. I keep that part to myself.

"Quit playing around." She gazes up at the ceiling in frustration.

Letting out a long sigh, I answer, "Yeah, so maybe I do like Nico. It isn't like I'm going to do anything about it, though. I don't even know if he likes me."

Straightening her body, she slides closer to me. "Well, you better, because his ex-girlfriend is here."

I still, my heart accelerating. Did I hear her correctly? I've never heard him talk about another girl or an ex-girlfriend. Jessie has never said anything either.

Grabbing Jessie's arm, I move her to the corner where no

one else is standing. "What do you mean ex-girlfriend? You never said he had a girlfriend *or* ex-girlfriend."

Jessie gets distracted by one of the paintings, and I snap my fingers in her face. "Yeah sorry"—she focuses back on me—"they broke up over the summer and had dated for three years. She used to come to the store all the time, like she had no other life besides hanging around at the sell or trade counter without getting paid. She's really nice, though. Violet told me she broke up with Nico because she's going away to college next year."

All I hear is that she was the one who broke up with him, and they broke up over the summer. That may be months ago, but three years is a long time to be dating someone. I haven't even dated someone for three days.

"Don't worry. He never seemed upset about it at work or anything." That doesn't help me, because I never seem upset at work about things either.

I can get over crushes. I have done it plenty of times. That's what I tell myself anyway.

"I'm okay, Jessie. Let's head back and find Violet. Did you see her artwork?" I try to look away from Jessie's face, so she doesn't see my let down expression. She moves to the side on purpose, so her face is still in mine.

Jessie stares at me like a worried parent and then snaps out of it. "No, I was too busy on a mission to find you. But, show me. I want to see this demon side of you." Taking hold of my shirt, she yanks me in Violet's direction.

We make our way to the front, then back down the art-filled hall until we find her. Violet introduces me to her and Nico's parents, Tim and Charlotte, who are standing with her.

They seem nice and proud of their daughter. Violet resembles her dad, while Nico looks a lot like his mom with the same auburn hair and honey-colored eyes.

I turn around and walk back to Jessie to show her Violet's drawings. We both stop in our tracks when we see Nico talking to a girl with long, curled, black hair. She's pretty and short with dark olive skin, but a lot of the girls are tiny next to me. She's taller than Violet, though, and she's standing close to him. My stomach drops, and I brush away the jealousy, invisibly holding up a white surrender flag. If he likes her, I will make myself be okay with that.

Sliding to the side, I attempt to sneak away. Nico and the girl have their backs facing away from us when Jessie blurts out, "Oh, May, you look so beautiful. Can a demon look beautiful? You definitely make demons look appealing."

Nico whirls around and gives us a big smile. *Damn it, Jessie.* The girl beside Nico turns around to us and smiles, too.

Nico strolls up beside me to introduce all of us. "Lanie, this is May and Jessie. I think you've met Jessie, but this is May. May, this is Lanie."

"Hey," I say in a small voice as I wave. What else can I say? I have a big, fake smile on my face. It's probably too big and resembles the Cheshire Cat.

"I love this picture of you and Nico," Lanie says while pointing at the drawing—she seems *nice*.

I nod. "Thanks. Violet was pretty intense that day."

Lanie laughs. "I agree. Violet can be determined with her art. One time I had to hold a flower and stand in the same position for what had to have been hours."

We all talk a while longer, and then Lanie tells us she's

leaving to meet up with some of her friends who are going to the movies. She's super nice, and I feel bad for getting all weirded out before. But I still have that sinking feeling in my stomach.

After we look at more of the artwork for a while longer, Nico walks us to the car to take us home. Jessie appears sulky in the backseat. "I'm still disappointed about the lack of interesting guys. Of course, the ones who I did think were cute already had girlfriends."

"What is she talking about?" Nico asks.

I roll my eyes. "Jessie is determined to find a college guy who will be on her level."

He lifts his hand from the steering wheel to change the radio station. "Oh, is that what you're looking for?" His gaze slides to mine, expression neutral, so I can't tell what he's thinking.

Pointing at myself, I quickly shake my head. "Me? No. She may be on that level, but I'm still a couple of levels below." His neutral expression grows into a smile.

We arrive at Jessie's house and she thanks us for inviting her. Technically, she was the one who invited herself, but I'd have most likely asked her to come. I would've ended up feeling bad for not inviting her.

Nico and I don't talk a lot on the drive to my house. He turns into my driveway and puts the car gear in park. His fingers tap the steering wheel, creating a miraculous private symphony. "What are you doing next Friday?"

I remember what Mom said about her going away. "My mom will be out of town for the week."

"Your mom is leaving you for the entire week?" Nico asks,

eyebrows rising all the way up.

"Yeah, but if I need anything, my next-door neighbor knows I'm alone. Well, she's more than a neighbor to us— I've known her my whole life."

Nico nods and reaches out to move a lock of hair from his face while chewing on the edge of his bottom lip. "Would you want to hang out on some of the days you have off from work? So, you won't get bored or anything."

My heart molds into an ice sculpture in my chest and doesn't move. "Sure. You'll have to come to my house, though. Mrs. Jenkins knows the days I have off from work, and she'll be eyeballing the house to make sure my car is at home. So, you'll need to park farther down the street." I can feel my whole body practically glowing.

Nico stops chewing his lip and grins. "Alright, I'll bring some movies."

"Sounds good, but you'll be watching a movie of mine first. Remember you still owe me from rock, paper, scissors when I first started work."

"Fine," he gives off a sarcastic huff.

I reach to open the car door when Nico blurts out, "No, wait right there." He hops out, runs around the car, and opens the remainder of the door for me.

I laugh. "Nico, it's one thing to open the door for me when I get into the car, but I don't have to wait in here for you to run around and open it for me."

He wipes his forehead in mock tiredness. "Good. We have that settled." I smile and find that every time he puts a smile on my face, I love it more and more. If I had the nerve, I'd kiss him at this moment, but I don't have that kind of courage.

Nico walks me to the doorway, and we stand there in silence. "Oh, can you also bring your guitar next week when you come over? I still haven't heard you play anything." I have been yearning to hear him play.

"Sure." He grins. "Well, I guess I'll see you tomorrow at work."

I shrug. "I guess so." I smile in return and half-turn to walk inside, but change my mind before facing him again.

I was holding back asking him about Lanie, but I have to find out. Now is the time, before I drive myself crazy. "So, Lanie doesn't mind if you come over?"

His eyebrows lower, almost fully connecting. "Lanie?"

"Yeah, I wasn't sure if you guys were together." I toss my hand down to my side in a weird attempt to appear like I don't care. It kind of looks like I'm shooting a basketball with one hand—it doesn't work.

A smile pulls to one side of Nico's face. "Oh? You thought Lanie and I were still together?"

Feeling nervous, I tug at my earlobe. "I don't know," I squeak. Now I'm *squeaking*?

"Well, we aren't." His gaze locks on mine, and his expression is serious.

"Okay," I say, and turn to walk to the front door, not wanting to sound too excited. Inside, however, I'm having my own little party.

Grabbing me by the arm, Nico stops me before I reach the door. "You probably already know she broke up with me over the summer, but we were over before that. I haven't felt that way for her in a while, and I should've been the one to break up with her sooner."

"Okay," I say again.

He gives me a knowing look.

*Whatever*, I think to myself. The party has turned into a full-blown concert in my chest, musical blowers and all.

I stare at him, and he continues to stare right back at me, apparently playing a game of who can stare the longest. I know I can win this game.

Unexpectedly, he leans forward and lowers his mouth to mine in a soft press of the lips. I'm shocked, my heart dancing, and even though I was hoping for this earlier, I didn't think it would happen.

He pulls back with an uncertain expression, and I look from his eyes to his nose and right back at those lips. Quickly, I move with hopefully not too much force, and I let my lips connect with his. His hand comes around to my back, drawing me closer.

Nico's tongue swipes against my bottom lip, prying my mouth open where his tongue then meets mine. My mouth moves gently against his while tugging him closer in our already non-existent space.

The kiss is everything I could've hoped for, and more. Nico is the first to pull away, and he rests his forehead against mine.

"I better go in." I say. "See you tomorrow at work?"

"See you tomorrow, May." He lifts his forehead off mine and slowly walks backward to his car—both of us smiling at the other—before turning around while I stand there watching him.

Walking inside, I beam brighter than the sun and shoot Jessie a text because I can't keep this a secret. It's too big.

Me: Nico and I kissed

Jessie: What??????

Me: I know!

# Chapter Ten

$\heartsuit$

Yesterday, I was busy working at the bookstore, constantly thinking about the kiss every time I looked at Nico. We grinned back and forth a lot, more than usual.

Today, I'm getting ready to hang out with Jessie before work, and Mom already left early this morning. She made sure she told me over and over not to let anyone into the house except for Jessie. As much as she likes Nico, no boys are allowed without her being present.

Nico is still going to come over to watch movies, though. What she doesn't know won't hurt her.

I leave the house and pick Jessie up at eight this morning. She yawns as she gets into the car. "When my alarm clock went off this morning, I had forgotten you wanted to go to the cemetery so early."

"It isn't that early," I say. "The sun is already out."

Jessie lets out another yawn. "True, but I'm still in vampire mode—I need to lie back down inside my coffin." Peering around the seat, she grabs the bag of supplies in the middle of the backseat. "Is this the stuff we need?"

Art has gotten me through a lot of the tough times. After Dad was buried, I became interested in gravestone rubbings. I haven't been to the cemetery to try it out, but I've wanted to for a long time now.

Today is that day.

"Hopefully." I wasn't sure how to do it, so I searched Google like I do everything else. The website said I'd need tape, rubbing wax, scissors, a spray bottle, rag, masking tape, soft brush, rubber bands, a large sheet of paper, and a poster tube. A lot of things.

Most of the stuff I already had around the house except for the rubbing wax, so I went to the store yesterday and bought that. I haven't been to the cemetery much since my dad passed. While I'm there, I figure I'll stop by and say hello.

The cemetery where Dad is buried has different ages of headstones—some are incredibly old with deterioration, and then others are on the newer side, all bright and shiny.

Jessie reaches to change the radio station while I'm driving. "So, your mom left for the week this morning? What are our plans? Party?" An expression of hope radiates across her face.

I shake my head. "No to the party. Nico is supposed to come over a couple of times this week."

"Shut up!" She shoves my arm. "Why did you not tell me this?"

"Well," I drawl, "it isn't like I tell someone every time you come over. It isn't a big deal." I shrug. "We plan to watch some movies."

Tilting her chin down, she gives me a stern look. "This is definitely a bigger deal than me coming over. Does Mother Dearest know this news?"

"No, Mom doesn't know," I say guiltily.

"May is turning into a rebel. Does this mean more kissing?" Jessie laughs.

I shove her shoulder, and she laughs even louder, causing my grin to spread.

When we pull up to the cemetery, there's one other car parked, but I don't see anyone around. If there were a funeral happening, we would have turned around and gone home.

First stop is my dad, and Jessie follows me to his resting spot. I locate his headstone and have a seat in the dew-covered grass. Taking a deep swallow, I close my eyes for a moment before reopening them. "Hello, Dad."

Jessie places her hand on my shoulder with a solemn expression. "I'll give you two time alone." She leaves to search for potential headstones to try some rubbings on.

The weather is perfect. The sun is shining brightly, and the sky is filled with puffy, white clouds. I stare at them for a few minutes. "Dad, remember when I used to think they were marshmallows?

"You told me they could be whatever I wanted them to be. Well, I wanted them to be marshmallows. Then you told me to reach for them, and maybe one day I would catch one. Every single day I would stretch my hand up to the sky until my elbow ached, and my hand came away with nothing.

"Finally, one day when I had my eyes closed and was wishing more than anything for a cloud, I caught one. It was one of those big, fluffy, cylinder-shaped ones. I know it was you who placed the marshmallow in my hand, but I was so ecstatic.

"It was only a regular marshmallow, but to me, it tasted better than any single one I had ever tasted. The marshmallow tasted like strong winds, warm sky, spring rain, and future dreams—all wrapped up in that perfect bite. Not that my younger self knew what those tasted like, but the possibilities were endless."

With the palms of my hands, I wipe away the warm tears that are streaming down my face. My eyes blur with new tears, and I use my arm to try and tuck those back in. "Thanks, Dad, for always helping my dreams become a reality. Wherever you are, I'll meet you on the other side one day."

I linger for a while longer like he's beside me, imagining us sitting there in silence as we always did, and it feels nice. There aren't enough words to describe how much I miss him, and I'm not mad anymore. I'm only glad he's no longer suffering the way he had been.

His headstone is directly in front of me, and I run my hands across the part where his name is engraved, telling him goodbye. I'm not ready to do a headstone rubbing on it today, but one day I will.

Gently, I walk through the grass, as if not to disturb any of the resting audience below. Jessie is already squatting and squinting at a headstone, reading what's written there.

She peers over at me with a close-lipped, welcoming smile—knowing she doesn't need to ask me if I'm okay because I get better with each passing day.

"I think I want to do this one." She points at a headstone directly across from her with a crack running up the side. Sprawled across the top are bird droppings and moss.

I pull out the spray bottle and brush and hand them to her. "These are to clean it, but be gentle when you do it."

The headstone is from the nineteen-forties, and I read the

rest while Jessie cleans it. It reads that Sarah Riddle was a wife and mother, and she died when she was only twenty-seven.

All the times I have visited Dad in the cemetery, I walked around and gave my company to others along the way—some of the older ones most likely don't have visitors anymore. Every time I read the headstones and see that people have died at early ages, I want to know the backstory of what happened or what the person was like.

If someone ever visits my dad's gravesite, they may think the same thing. The answer won't ever come, though.

Fishing out another brush and spray bottle from the bag, I begin working on a headstone next to Jessie's. This one has the name Joseph Riddle, and he died at age seventy-four. It most likely is Sarah's husband. That's a long time to live without his wife, but they're together now.

"Okay, I think I got it clean enough." Jessie sighs and sets the supplies down. "The top needed it. The cemetery owners should really hire someone to make sure these stones stay clean. I wouldn't want bird crap on my house."

I start to put away my water bottle and brush. "Your house?"

"Yes! These spots are their homes forever, so they should be taken care of," she exclaims.

She does have a point. Locating the large roll of paper, I hand her a piece. We fold ours both over our headstone and tape it off in the back, so it doesn't fall off onto the ground.

Kneeling to find the bag, I locate both pieces of wax and hand Jessie one. "Next time we can try it with crayon, but I wanted to use the wax this time."

Nodding, she watches me as I start to get the hang of what

to do. It's easy, and anyone could do it. I rub mine for a while longer than Jessie, so I can achieve the exact shaded depth I'm looking for. I love doing this. Sketching, coloring, painting— I can get consumed by it all when I work, and when I finish, my heart feels full.

Stepping back, Jessie examines her work. "I may not be an artist, but I feel like one today."

She took an art class with me in ninth grade. It was the first time she'd ever tried it, and it was also her last time. Every time she would do a project, Mrs. Burke would come and observe her.

Mrs. Burke was picky, but she was even pickier with Jessie's art. She'd squint only one eye, and it made it look like she was giving Jessie's stuff the stink eye—she might've been.

She would take the picture out of Jessie's hand and start sketching or painting it herself, depending on what we were doing that day. Mrs. Burke even started molding the whole project for her when we worked with clay. Jessie may not have been great, but she wasn't *that* bad.

After that, she was done with art until she took up photography sophomore year. We did some cool projects where she'd take a picture, and I would draw it. Jessie said we could make our own exhibit with these projects of real-life photographs and drawings together. Of course, Jessie got tired of photography and moved on, while I still love art as I always have.

Carefully, we take our paper down from the headstones to roll them up, and I hand Jessie a rubber band. I wrap my band around the paper gently, making sure it isn't too tight, and then place it in the tube.

I grab my bag from the ground, and we walk back to the car. There are two new cars parked, and an elderly woman is stepping out of one of them—most likely to visit a loved one. "Thanks for coming with me today," I say. "Not only to do the stone rubbings, but to be here with me."

She shifts closer to me and wraps her arm around my shoulder. "You know I'm always here for you, May. Now, I need you to help me, though."

We stop in front of the car. "Oh, yeah? What do you need help with this time?"

She has that "in love" expression on her face. "The new guy that started at work yesterday…"

Letting out a long sigh, I draw my hand up to pinch the bridge of my nose. "Don't tell me you're already crushing on John."

This guy already seems like bad news and probably won't even last a week. He has long, black hair that falls right below his shoulders, and he's lazy. He's also in a band which is the only good part. I know when Jessie heard the word *band*, that's what did it.

Her head hits the back of the seat with a dreamy expression. "Yes, and he's in a band. *The drums.*"

I might not be so quick to write him off if he didn't take a smoke break every thirty minutes, ignoring the only two fifteen-minute breaks he's supposed to have. Not to mention, he kept straining to read the print on the book covers to put them in the correct places.

I asked him if he needed to get glasses, and he said he had them at home but never wears them. If he needs them to do his job, then he needs to wear them.

"I'll offer you a deal. If you pick out any other guy, I'll be all for it." I'd go and find him right now for her.

Jessie scratches the side of her hand, contemplating. "I don't know, but I'll think about it."

After I drop Jessie off at her house, I drive home before I've got to head into work. I step into the art room that's now only mine and set the tube from the cemetery against the wall.

I haven't gone in here since Dad died, but I feel like I'm finally able to.

# Chapter Eleven

♡

Mom calls me from Uncle Jim's all week.

She went to the doctor with Uncle Jim on Wednesday and found out he has high blood pressure and will start taking a pill to help lower it. I'm relieved that it's only high blood pressure, and not something worse.

His house was a pigsty when Mom arrived, and she has spent the last several days cleaning up the disaster. I have a feeling he won't keep up with the housework once Mom leaves.

It hasn't been bad staying by myself at home. I've gone to Mrs. Jenkins' place every day, eating an early dinner there after school. She practically insisted on me staying each night, but I declined her request each time, telling her if I changed my mind I would come right over.

Nico stopped by on Tuesday and Wednesday, and both days we watched movies. I picked first, and then he chose a zombie movie that's part of a three-part series. We didn't talk about anything serious—we mostly talked along with the movies, as if we were the characters. We made it through the first two zombie movies, but each time after finishing the films before he left, we kissed for a long time on the couch, and I didn't want him to leave.

We finish our shift at around nine tonight, and Nico is coming over directly after. He's bringing over the final zombie film, and I'm ready for it.

"Should I stop by the store and pick up anything on the way to your house?" he asks, fishing his keys out of his pocket.

I grab mine and unlock the door. "If you want chips. You finished the whole bag on Wednesday. Otherwise, we're good."

Nico bumps his shoulder against mine. "I distinctly remember you eating more chips than I did."

"Maybe?" I say and shift my eyes to the side as I smile.

Leaning forward, he gives me a quick brush of the lips before heading to open his car door. "I'll be there in a while."

"Park away from the house like you have been." I don't need Mrs. Jenkins giving a report to my mom.

When I get home, the house is bathed in darkness, so I flip on both lamps and turn on the TV to sit down and watch it for a while.

*Tap-tap-tap.* The knock is soft, and I rush to the door to open it. Clenching Nico's shirt, I pull him inside before Mrs. Jenkins has a chance to see him. It looks like she went to bed already because there weren't any lights on when I got home.

My stomach dips at the sight of him. Nico has two big plastic bags in his hand, and he hands me one. I take it and dig inside, finding one of those huge tubs of cheese balls, plain chips, and multiple dips. I pull out the container of cheese balls. "You know I could marry you for bringing these."

"Oh yeah?" he asks, arching a brow. Quickly, I turn and walk to the couch, drawing my face up in a wince that's filled with embarrassment. *Why did I say that?*

I try to play it off. "Yeah, but only if you brought me a container every single day for the rest of our lives."

Nico scratches his head and laughs. "Only if you give me those juice boxes you have for the rest of *your* life." He removes the guitar that's strapped on his back and places it beside the couch, before following me into the kitchen.

Laughing, I walk to the fridge, grabbing us both orange flavored juice boxes. He unwraps the plastic off his straw, pokes it in the hole of the juice box, instantly taking a sip. Realizing I'm focused on his lips, I tear my eyes away from his mouth.

I turn my stare to the guitar case, leaning against the couch. "So, I see you brought your guitar this time. Are you ready to play for me?"

He lets out a huff that shows he's only pretending he doesn't want to do it. "If you want me to." He's already reaching for the case and drawing out his acoustic guitar.

I sink down on the couch, waiting in anticipation. "You've postponed this long enough, Nico. I'm all ears."

He strums the strings and plays a song for me with a slow tempo, building gradually. My heart thrums along as though it's listening too. I feel connected to it, watching the way his fingertips press against the chords—the way his other hand holds the pick and strums—the way his auburn head is tilted down, holding the bottom edge of his lip between his teeth. His eyes draw to mine and hold, and I don't look away.

Nico ends the song, and I'm impressed. "Now, I know you're good. You have officially entered the category of moving the needle out of the middle and toward the section that reads 'good.'"

"I showed you mine, now you have to show me yours." Nico grins, tilting his head back at me while bending over his case to place the guitar inside.

I have no idea what he's talking about. "Um." I just stare at him.

His responding grin is huge. "Your art, dummy. What did you think I was talking about?"

Oh. He wants to see my art. I never had a problem letting anyone see my art before, but showing him somehow feels different—like I'm exposing myself to him. I think about it, and I like the idea of that. "Sure. You have to come with me, though."

"Now, I'm intrigued." Nico props his case back against the couch and follows behind me to the art room.

Opening the door, I step into the room. I've been coming in here all week, working on sketches for art class. "This is the art room. Some of my drawings are over there." I point to a desk covered in piles of pencils, charcoal, paints, and markers.

Nico glances at my desk, then turns his head to the other desk against the other wall. "What about that?"

I study my feet for a minute, knowing what Nico is staring at. "That was all my dad's art and supplies. He was the one who taught me everything he knew."

He looks at a big piece that my dad painted of Mom and me when I was around six. The colors he used are all wild and bright and not the normal colors of our skin or hair. It represents the way he saw us, and how we always brightened everything in his life more than it was. That's what he told me anyway.

Nico glances at me over his shoulder. "He was really good." Then he goes back to studying the painting.

I decide to tell him what happened. Nico has become more than a co-worker—he's a good friend and becoming so much more.

I walk and stand next to him, gazing at the painting. "My dad died from cancer." I turn to look at his face. He's staring at me intently, and I focus back on the painting of Mom and me. "All the time in movies and books, there's always someone dying from cancer. I used to ask myself 'why can't they choose another illness? They always choose cancer.'" I pause. "It's because cancer affects so many damn people. My dad waited until it was too late. He wouldn't go to the doctor to find out what was wrong. All he had to do was seek help, but then you see so many people go through the treatments and lose every ounce of themselves and still die in the end. Maybe that was also what he was afraid of. I only wish he would've tried before it was considered terminal."

Before I have a chance to react, Nico pulls me into an embrace. My head falls against his shoulder, and I stand there for a long time holding onto him. He doesn't say anything and doesn't have to, but I do. "He didn't just die—he shot himself in his room while we were here."

His arms tighten around me, and he curses softly. I step back and tell him everything, emotions pouring out of me in crashing waves, as he listens. After I finish, I transition awkwardly to a new subject. "So, my drawings and stuff are over there."

I pad to my desk and hand him my sketchbook. He takes it with interest and immediately flips through it. It's filled with mainly fantasy creatures, monsters, and my version of creepy flowers. I like to do real-life drawings, too, but there's just something about sketching things you don't see on a normal basis.

He uses his time to absorb each picture. "These are really good, May. Are you sure you don't want to try to pursue art as a career somehow?" His head lifts to me quickly before turning back to the pictures.

"No way. I like having it as a hobby. As much as I love it, I would much rather teach it. I don't have the drive your sister has to show my work or make art for other people. Violet has the personality along with the art, and it will take her somewhere."

I couldn't do all that. It's mainly a release for myself when I'm having a stressful day, inspired, or even bored—I escape and live through it.

I pull out a couple of paintings, leaning against the wall and show him. They're abstract—he can decide whatever he wishes them to be.

"Are you going to draw a picture of me?" Tilting his chin down, he looks me dead-on in the eye.

"Do you want me to draw a picture of you?" I smile. "I know you're used to it from Violet." I'd like to sketch him. At work when I used to try and hide that I was seriously looking at him, I wished I had a pencil and my sketchbook right there.

He tilts his head to the side "Yeah, I want to see your real-life skills."

"Okay." Feeling excited and nervous at the same time, I grab another book I have that has drawings of people only. I bring it into my room with a pencil, since I like the lighting in here better than the living room. Before I begin sketching, I turn on the movie and sit on the bed. Nico sits down beside me against the headboard and watches the TV. I lean forward and draw a side profile picture of his face.

My hand shakes at first from the nerves bubbling through my body from staring at him, but I quickly realize I'm drawing, so it's okay to stare. We may have already kissed three times, but the nervousness hasn't faded. I scoot closer to him to get the details as accurate as possible for the lines of his jaw and nose. He turns his head to say something, and I guess he didn't realize my face had gotten so close. I smile and casually move back.

Nico gently grabs my arm and stops me from drifting away. His gaze falls to my lips, and I don't want to wait until after the movie for us to kiss tonight.

Setting down my drawing stuff, I lift my hands to grasp his face, bringing my lips softly to his. Slowly, I sail my lips across his, and it feels more than spectacular, better than seeing a shooting star.

This is when he takes the kiss into real kiss territory. He opens his lips and caresses his mouth against mine with firmer pressure. It's more than a kiss. It's a rain dance filled with twirling, rain, lightning, and storms. My heart thunders against my ribcage, and I don't want the feeling to ever end. Not today and not tomorrow.

Our kisses so far have been amazing, but this kiss, this kiss holds the power to unlock everything inside me, and the key is all his. I want it, and I want more of him. I swipe my tongue across his lower lip like he usually does to me before brushing my tongue against his.

He starts to lie back and pulls me on top of him as I thread my hands through his hair and tug gently. His hands run over the edge of my shirt, and he slowly drags it up, stopping midway, as if questioning me if it's all right. And it's so all right. Leaning forward, I let him peel it all the way off. We kiss and we kiss, until there needs to be more—there *must* be more. The rest of our clothes come off piece by slow piece, falling to the floor in a broken puzzle.

Nico rolls me to my back and hovers above me. He pulls back from my lips, trailing kisses along my jaw to my ear, and I tug him closer to me.

Lifting his head from my ear, he chews the edge of his lip while peering down at me. "We can stop right now."

"I don't want to. Do you?" I ask. At this moment it feels right, and I don't want to stop.

He leans back to get a better look at my eyes. "I don't want to stop, but it may not be good." He glances away and says, "I haven't done this before."

Did he think I was a pro at this? Then it hits me. "You mean, you and Lanie didn't? After three years?" I'm stunned by this. Three years is a long time.

Shaking his head, his face holds an emotion I haven't seen from him. "No. It's different with you than it was with her."

I press my lips to his again. "I haven't been with anyone either. We'll have to figure it out together."

He smiles. "I didn't think you had, but I wasn't sure."

There's a lot of laughing with the awkwardness of it all being new, until it all comes together. It hurts, and it may not be perfect, but it's perfection to me.

We fall asleep afterward, and I wake to Nico still sleeping.

Slowly, he opens his eyes and gives me a sleepy grin. "This means you're my girlfriend now, right?"

"Maybe." I smile. I've been waiting for him to bring it up, and now I don't think the smile will ever shut off.

Nico reaches his hands out, his fingers at my sides, and then he tickles me until I can't take it. "Yes! Yes, it does. Now quit," I half-cry and half-laugh.

# Chapter Twelve

♡

*S*ix weeks have passed since I first slept with Nico. Since then, we slowed things down a little, but not too much. He's been awesome. Life was running perfect, until today. Now, Jessie comes over and gives me bad news to add to my stack of horrible events in life.

"What do you mean you're moving?" I cry out.

Tears are flowing down Jessie's face. "Dad said his work has transferred him to Hawaii. It would be awesome if we went on a vacation there, but I don't want to be isolated on that tiny island away from everything!"

I lean against the wall in the hallway, wanting to slap it with the palm of my hand. "You can't move! You're my best friend!"

"I know! I don't want to start a new school during my junior year. And what about John?" She runs her hand through her blonde hair that she recently colored back from the orange and yellow.

"What about him?" I demand.

"He's finally starting to notice me. He asked me to come watch his band!"

I was wrong about John. A tad bit. He's lasted more than

a week at the store.

I don't want to burst Jessie's bubble, but John asked everyone at work to watch his band.

We talk for a while longer about her moving and tell each other that we will talk every day. Reaching into her purse, she hands me a small bag. It's the reason she came over today.

I take the bag from her, pull out the box, and stare at the pregnancy test.

I don't know the exact day I was supposed to start my period, but it's late, and I grew beyond worried. I talked to Jessie, and she told me she'd bring a test over.

Nico and I were both so stupid and caught up in that moment. I didn't think about condoms, and he didn't either. Afterward, he did talk to me about it, and he'd make sure he had one if we decided to do it again. I wasn't worried since it had only happened once. Next time, we'd be prepared.

Now here I am, with the king of condoms laughing and shaking his finger at me for not using one. I walk into the bathroom and pee on the stick. I'm not going to wait for the results in the hallway. Instead, I stand in the bathroom holding the edge of the stick clenched in my fist, watching it like a hawk eyeballing its food with full-blown intensity.

I don't know how much time has passed, but the result is there now. *Pregnant.* These are the sticks with no confusing lines—the results show up pregnant or not pregnant. I throw the stick on the floor so hard that the plastic cracks, and the sound echoes. I pick it up to hide in the trash, so Mom doesn't see it.

There's a light knock on the door. "Are you alright? It doesn't sound so good in there." Jessie's voice is practically a whisper.

"That's because it isn't!" I yell.

I'm not even crying. I'm not upset. I don't know what I am. I'm angry that out of my whole life, I was only truly stupid this one time, and we'd planned to fix that for all the future times. I'm scared to tell Mom. I'm worried about the future now. What is Nico going to say? Is he going to be pissed? I need to stop. I'm going to puke everywhere.

I open the door a little too hard, and Jessie jumps back. "I have to talk to Nico."

Stomping down the hall, I find my purse, keys, and phone. I shoot Nico a text.

Me: I'm stopping by work. Save your break for me.

Nico: Anything for you.

I don't reply with a smart aleck remark like I generally do. "Jessie, I'll come by your house after I talk to Nico. Is that okay?"

She nods solemnly. "Anytime. I'm here, alright?"

Yeah, she'll be here until she moves to Hawaii. I've been stabbed in the chest twice today. Am I being dramatic? I don't think so.

Driving to work a little faster than normal, I park in an open space beside Nico's car and get out to slam the door. Then I silently tell my car I'm sorry. It isn't its fault I'm an idiot.

I run through the parking lot like I'm trying to beat the sand pouring from the hourglass, hair flapping and slapping me in the face. Yanking open the door, I spot Nico right away. I must look like someone died because Nico stops what he's doing and hurries toward me. "What's wrong?"

I tug on the sleeve of his shirt. "Can you come outside?"

Nico walks toward John and asks him to take over counter duty. He moves an auburn lock of hair to the side of his forehead, and I wish I would've been the one to move it. Screw that. I'm pissed at him and pissed at me.

We hurry outside and sit on the bench outside the store. "What's goin—"

"I'm pregnant," I blurt.

Nico stares at me, furrowing his brow, clearly confused about what I'm saying. "Sorry? I don't understand."

My eyes grow wide, and I slap my hands against my knees. "What do you mean, you don't understand? We slept together, remember? It was my first time, and I didn't even think about a condom. You didn't say anything either!"

"It was my first time, too! I didn't think to bring a whole roll of condoms to your house when I didn't know it was going to happen!" he whisper-shouts.

"Well, you could've at least brought one!" I shoot him a glare.

He settles back against the bench. "Okay, so we both could've planned things differently. But are you sure? I mean are you sure here?" His face is full of hope like I'm going to tell him this is all a big joke. Well, I'm not.

The glare I'm giving him slides away. I lean against the bench, resting my shoulder against Nico's bicep and let out a sigh. "Yes. I just took a test." Tears prick my eyes.

Nico releases a string of curses, and on any other day I would laugh, but this is no laughing matter.

"We'll figure something out. If I have to work more than I already do, I will." Nico's face has gone pale, and his hands are fidgeting. He looks more worried than I do with his twitching hands, even though I'm the one who will have the growing stomach that everyone will be able to see. "I'm not going to lie, I'm freaking out inside."

Circling my arms around his waist, I try and give him a little comfort, but how can I offer that when my whole life is going to be ruined? "I'm beyond freaked out, Nico. And now Jessie is moving, too. I won't have anyone."

"What? Jessie is moving?"

"Yes, to Hawaii," I sob.

Pulling me close, he lifts my chin to study my face. "Look, I'm not angry at you. I'm pissed at myself for not having a condom, but I'm not the type who walks away from something because the circumstances have taken the worst turn possible. I'm not going to leave you alone in this. Ever. Alright?" I don't want to think about him not being with me through this, and I hope he isn't one who will leave me hanging through this situation by myself.

"I'm going to let Mom know first," I mumble into his shirt. She's going to be pissed beyond recognition.

We sit on the bench outside until he silently walks back into work. We're both struggling with our thoughts.

After I leave Nico at the bookstore, I stop by Jessie's house. She's still a loaded mess with tears flying everywhere and shouting at nothing. I try to calm her down, and she tries to give me advice about how to tell Mom, but we are both stuck in our heads. The pregnancy should be a bigger issue for me, but I feel like if she's here with me instead of in Hawaii, it will make the process somewhat more bearable. Even though it isn't.

I then head home, knowing Mom will be back from the grocery store where she was when Jessie came over earlier. Some teenagers hide their pregnancies for months, holding that burden in. I can't do that to myself or my mom. I'm going to be honest with her, as scared shitless as I am.

"What do you mean you're pregnant?" she screeches so loud the walls must have cracked.

I now wish I could take the whole *honesty is the best policy* thing back and crawl into a hole and hibernate.

"How could you do this? Did you even use protection?" she groans. "You better tell me you used protection!" Her teeth grind back and forth.

Shame fills my entire skeletal system. No matter how awkward "the talks" were, she always told me to make sure the guy wrapped it up.

"I-I didn't think about it."

She slams her hands against the old, laminate countertop. "You didn't think about it? Well, you're thinking about it now, aren't you?"

Pressing my hands against my forehead, I drag them so slowly down my face that skin must be peeling away with them. "Yes, Mom. I was an idiot, and Nico was an idiot. We both know." A few tears stream down my face, and I quickly wipe them away.

Mom straightens. "Oh, you bet your butt I'm going to have a sit down with Nico, followed by his parents. That boy isn't going to be one of those morons like on those teenage shows on TV who thinks it's all fine and dandy and then leaves the girl in the dust. He's going to step up the game here." She flings her arms wildly all over the place.

She points her finger at me. "And, don't you think for a second I'm going to raise this baby, you're going to have to step up your game, too. This baby is all on you, whatever you decide."

Defeat washes over me. "I know."

She sighs in frustration with anger continuing to roll off her in waves. "I'm not going to let you give up on college either. If you have to do night school or online courses, whatever it takes. You will amount to something. Do you hear me?"

I don't normally hug my mom, but I walk toward her, wrapping my arms around her and sob. Right when she has finally started to become Mom again, I go and pull this stunt. The past month she has improved so much because of the counselor's help. "I love you, and I'm so sorry."

"I love you, too, May. But I'm extremely pissed, and things are going to be different around here." Her face is pulled down into the hardest frown I've ever seen in my life.

I may not know a lot about babies, but from the few I've been around, I know they're a lot of work. They are always needy, little creatures—my life is officially over.

Mom has me text Nico to come here as soon as he gets off work. When she found out we were together, she was the happiest person in the universe. If anyone is Nico's biggest fan, it's her. I guess not anymore.

I type Nico a quick text.


Me: Can you come over after work? Mom wants to talk to you.

Nico: Uh-oh

Yes. Big uh-oh.

♥

The doorbell rings, signaling Nico's arrival. I start to rise off the couch to answer, but Mom stops me when I'm halfway off the seat. "Don't even think about it. You stay there." She points at me, and I feel like I'm seven years old again.

Opening the door, Mom smiles a huge fake smile. "Nico, why don't you have a seat on the couch next to May," she spits out.

Nico shifts his gaze from Mom to me, looking unsure what to do, even though she told him to come sit down on the couch. Then he finally makes a move, heading to sit beside me but not too close.

Mom shuts the door, a bit too loud, and walks until she's standing directly in front of us, then turns to Nico. "Nico, we aren't going to sit here and play games. We all know it takes two to tango." I cringe when she says this.

Nico's mouth starts to open, and Mom puts up the alligator hand and chomps it shut. "I'm not going to yell anymore. I already did that with May. I know how relationships work, especially young relationships. This may not last in the long run—most high school relationships don't. I'm not trying to hurt either of you, just being honest here. But my duty as May's mom is to make sure that regardless of what happens, you're going to be here for this baby."

Nico's throat bobs. "Yes, ma'am. I would never abandon May or this baby."

Mom sighs. "You don't know the future, Nico, but for today I've had enough of this already. We're going to talk about what's going to happen next."

Mom explains to Nico the proper use of a condom, and it's embarrassing. She's still angry and upset and probably will be forever. Then she goes in her room, slams the door, and gives us time to ourselves to sort things out.

Nico pulls my hand into his. "This situation is a mess, but I wouldn't just get up and walk away."

Thinking about what my mom said, I hope he wouldn't. Even if something happened to us, I hope he'd help raise the baby. The Nico who I have come to know would always be there in some way.

# Chapter Thirteen

After talking to Nico a little more about the baby situation, Mom stomps out of her room still fuming. She's forcing us to tell Nico's parents right away. She said there's no use procrastinating, and she isn't going to do the dirty work for us. Her last words are, "You better believe I will speak with them once you two have spilled the beans."

Nico then gives me a ride to his house. I'm more worried about telling his parents than I was my mom. I have gotten to know them over the last six weeks, and I like them a lot.

When we get there, Violet has just gotten home from work. Nico walks toward her at the table. "Where's Mom and Dad?"

She's sitting at the kitchen table eating chips, dipping them into a jar of cheese. "They'll be back soon. They went out to eat for dinner."

"You didn't go?" His eyebrows furrow, almost hitting each other.

"No. I wasn't in the mood for Italian." She takes a bite of her chip that's more cheese than anything.

"Oh." Nico turns to me. "Do you want to tell her, or wait to tell Mom and Dad?"

Violet sets the chip down on her napkin, scrunching up her

nose like she smells something bad. "Something is fishy here. You two aren't running off to get married, are you?"

"No!" we say simultaneously. Why would we be doing that?

She picks up the chip again, as if all things are solved. "Thank all that is holy for that."

Nico sits in a chair, and I slump down beside him, giving him the nod to go ahead. "She's having a baby, though."

Violet stares at us like she doesn't understand, and then her eyelids become non-existent. "What!" she shouts, dropping her chip on the floor. "Shit!" She leans over to pick it back up.

Taking over full parental mode, she yells for about five minutes straight. Nico seems lost as his lips part, and I can tell he hasn't ever seen Violet so angry. Her face has the reddest tint I've ever seen on a person. It kind of makes me want to hide under the table and never surface again.

I didn't know her reaction was going to be worse than my own mother's. "Your lives are officially over—do you know that?" She slams her hands on the table, causing it to rattle.

"Drop it, Violet! You don't even know!" Nico yells.

"I don't know? No, I don't know, because I was smart enough not to get pregnant!" She points her finger right at Nico's chest across the table.

Oh. That burns. Nico rolls his eyes. "That's not fair! You don't even date guys!"

This is true. Violet is into girls, so there's no chance of pregnancy happening there anytime soon. I don't want to get into it, so I stay silent like a shadow.

Violet straightens in her seat, as if it's her own personal throne. "It's the smartest decision I've ever made in my entire life, too.”

Letting out a long sigh, she then speaks again, “Look, I know you two are babies, but you should’ve researched how to do things correctly.”

“I’m not a baby, Violet. You’re only two years older than me,” Nico says drily.

“By age, yes.” She taps her finger against her head. “Mentally, it’s a different story.”

Nico throws back his chair and stands. “I think we’re done here.”

“Drop the attitude and sit down. Have you two decided to keep the baby?” Violet’s face turns into one of concern.

Nico and I haven’t discussed it, but I assumed we would. Some people are fine with other options, but I want to keep the baby. Nico nods at me, and we’re silently in agreement.

“We’re keeping the baby,” I say.

“I’m not going to argue with what you guys want to do, but at least you have that part settled. This may be too soon, but I’m always two steps ahead. I will offer to help babysit. Not that I’m a big baby fan, but I know how hard things are going to be. Trust me, I’ve seen friends go through this, and I don’t ever want to go through it myself.” Violet shudders.

She seems to have calmed down, and I’m surprised by her babysitting offer so soon after we told her, but it is Violet. She tends to think ahead, like she said.

Nico’s parents pull into the driveway at that moment. Pushing her chair back, Violet steps away from the table. “I have no intentions of watching this, but do know I will be listening from my room.” She takes off without another word.

My hands shake, and Nico takes one in between his and

holds it. "We'll get through this, okay?" His tone isn't as solid as I hoped for it to be, but it's more level than mine would sound.

Charlotte and Tim walk through the door looking as if they're happy teenagers who went out on their first date together.

I've been around them a lot since I started dating Nico. Every weekend we have dinner and play games together—either a board game or charades.

Charlotte lays her purse on top of the counter. "Hey, May. I didn't know you were going to grace us with your lovely presence today."

"Hey, Charlotte." I wave. I think I'm going to be the mute mouse throughout this moment. I'm panicking on the inside, and I may hyperventilate waiting to break the news.

Nico pulls my hand with his onto the table and leans forward. "Mom, we need to talk to you."

His mom glances at him and quickly blinks about ten times, and her smile erodes into a biting of the lip that then decays into lips pursed extremely tight. "This isn't what I think it is, is it? Please tell me it isn't, Nico."

Nico rubs his hand across his jaw. "I don't know? What do you think it is?"

"Nicolai Jonah! Don't sit here and play games with me. This isn't a quiz." She turns her head to me and shrieks, "Are you pregnant?"

Nico's dad walks into the kitchen and stops in place. "Fuck!" The normally laid back and quiet Tim is no longer that way in this precise moment.

There's a snicker down the hall, and I know Violet is as

surprised as I am about her dad.

"Enough, Violetta!" Charlotte yells, then whips her head back to us.

I want to open my mouth and speak, but my eyes are shifting back and forth between Nico's parents. Am I paralyzed? I think I am.

"Yes, she is," Nico speaks for me, his shoulders hunched, defeated.

Nico's mom cries, and Tim lets out a string of curses. Some of the words I never knew existed in the way that he uses them. Tim composes himself and walks to Charlotte, wrapping his arm around her to calm her, but he silently gives Nico the evil eye.

After watching Charlotte cry and slowly wipe away her tears, we begin the talk. Well, mainly Nico gets yelled at, and I don't know if it's because he's a guy or that he's their son. It's equal parts our fault, so I feel like I should be getting as much of a yelling as Nico.

Tim pulls Nico to the side to have his own private chat with his son. Charlotte walks around the table and sits beside me, and I'm scared shitless to look at her in the eye. "Look, we all make mistakes in life. I wish you two would've been a lot older, but there's nothing we can do now except move forward. Have you two considered the options, and what might be best here?" Her mouth pulls down into a frown.

Slowly, I nod. "Yes, ma'am. We're going to keep the baby."

She nods in return with a grim expression. "I need to yell at my son now, but if you need to talk, I'm here."

I sit by myself in silence, not knowing how I'm going to

get through this once the baby is here and becomes a real
reality.

# Chapter Fourteen

♡

*I*'m already three and a half months pregnant. Mom is still pissed but has been researching baby stuff and what stores have things the cheapest. She's already planning a baby shower months down the road and not for the pure enjoyment.

She said she might be embarrassed that her seventeen-year-old daughter is pregnant, but she isn't embarrassed enough to not have a shower and make sure all the cheapskates at her work give a gift.

Nico is with me in my room with the door open, while Mom is watching TV. I don't see why the door has to be open, since I'm already in the situation that could occur with a closed door. Mom's rules, though.

Pulling Nico's arm toward me, I roll the sleeve of his shirt all the way up. I quickly kiss his bicep, and he gives me a wide smile. "What do you want me to draw?" I ask.

"You're the one who wanted to draw on my arm." He slides my hair away from my face.

"Okay, I'll think of something." I settle on drawing a bundle of balloons.

"I'm not going to get ink poisoning from that pen, am I?" he jokes.

"No." I hope not. Pen ink washes right off. Do people

really get ink poisoning from a ballpoint pen? I haven't known anyone personally who has before. I use a pen on myself all the time at school to write down the classes I have homework for on the top of my hand. Otherwise, I won't remember.

I wish Mom wasn't home as I grip Nico's arm, his warmth radiating into me. Placing the pen against his arm, my stomach flutters as I sketch. "I have an important question."

"What's that?" His beautiful face turns toward mine.

I concentrate on his arm. "Have you thought about names?"

"For the baby?"

"Yes, for the baby," I say. "Who else?"

"No." He laughs. "Why, have you?"

Finishing the fifth balloon, I tie them together with a small line that resembles a rubber-band, then start on a balloon flying away from the bundle. "Of course I have."

"What do you got? I'm not too picky as long as it isn't some out there name, but I do like originality," he says.

I stall the pen and look at him. "I narrowed it down to three boy names and three girl names. Maybe you can pick out one from each set."

"What if I hate them all?" He grins.

"Then, I guess I'll have to make a new list." I laugh.

Tugging me into his lap, he lies me back against his firm chest. "Start with the boy names."

Boy names were the most difficult to come up with. I don't know what it is, but I could only come up with three. If he hates all three names, then he'll have to come up with them himself.

I researched for hours. A name might not seem like a big

deal, but you have to live with that thing for your entire life. Then when I was researching and trying to think of names, it was like the same terrible name kept popping up in my head over and over, like that was the only name that existed.

"So, for the boys I have, Journey, River, and Forest," I say proudly.

"I guess we're going to take a journey through the river in a forest." Nico chuckles loudly like he's invented the greatest joke ever made.

I sit there and frown. "I thought they were good."

"Pass on Journey. Pass on Forest. I can do River, though. It sounds solid enough."

"What's wrong with Journey and Forest?" I pout.

Nico lightly flicks my arm. "You know what is wrong with the two. Do we need people to bust out in song all the time to the poor child or ask him about chocolate?"

I cross my arms. "Forrest Gump. Really? The spelling would've been different, and I doubt anyone would even think of that. But fine. River works."

Nico makes a drumroll with his fingers against my headboard, and it vibrates through him into my back. "And the girl names are?"

The girl names were much easier. I had a list of about fifty, and it took me forever to narrow them down to three, but I managed to do it. If he hates all three, it will be much easier to go back to that list and give him some more names.

"After much deliberation, I came up with Charlotte—"

"I'm going to stop you right now and remove Charlotte from the list. I can't go through life getting confused between the baby's name and my mother's." His warm breath brushes against my ear.

"But I like Charlotte," I whine. Charlotte's a great name, and I love it.

"Veto."

I let out a grunt but proceed. "Daisy or Ruby."

Nico's arms tighten around my stomach. "I'm not going to be reminded about a cartoon duck every time either."

"Not like the duck! The flower!"

"Veto!"

"Whatever. Fine," I mumble.

"I don't quite understand what you said." He grins widely.

I ignore him. "What about Ruby? Do you not like that one either?" I huff.

"No, I like that one." Nico kisses the side of my neck.

"Me, too." Thank goodness for that, because Ruby is my favorite.

Crawling out of his arms, I find the pen I dropped somewhere on the bed, then continue drawing the balloons on his arm. I feel like they need a little color, so I reach for my box of markers and pick out different colors for each balloon. But I find it hard to keep my eyes from drifting up to Nico's beautiful face.

# Chapter Fifteen

♡

*N*ico asked me to go to prom with him. Of course, I said yes at the time because I was only two months along. I didn't think ahead to when prom was, or that at four and a half months pregnant, I would feel like I was already nine months along.

My stomach was already slightly noticeable, especially in the dress I picked out a month ago. I'd been around the same size I'd always been and then the other day out of nowhere, the ball on my stomach shot forward.

I ordered this fifties style, blue and white polka-dotted dress that's tight on top and flares out on the bottom. Mom curled my hair and pinned it up in a vintage style, and I applied my make-up myself.

"Ruby, I'm going to make sure you don't follow in my footsteps. Do you hear me? There will be zero boys in your life until after you're at least out of high school," I whisper at my stomach while rubbing a hand across the material of the dress.

We found out earlier this week that the baby is going to be a girl, and Nico almost passed out. He said boys were easier not to worry about as much, and now he says he's going to get gray hairs before he's twenty-five.

I'm doing everything I can with school and work to make Ruby's life okay. I know it isn't a lot, but most of my money is going straight into savings for whatever we might possibly need. Mom recently got a raise at work, but I'm determined to do it myself without making it more of a burden on her than it already will be. It doesn't feel real besides the progressions of my growing stomach, but when the baby arrives, that's when everything will change.

I gaze at myself in the mirror, and a few tears stream down my face. I try to hold them back so I don't mess up my makeup, but I can't help it. Instead of appearing like a beautiful girl from a different era, I look more like the housewife who got knocked up by the milkman. Except I'm a seventeen-year-old girl, not the cheating wife.

The doorbell rings and Mom calls my name, "May! Come on. Nico's waiting." But I just stand here.

"May, come on!" I leave my room after she calls me down a second time. Mom grips her huge camera in one hand, and the camera on her phone in the other—both ready to take pictures.

After my gaze stops getting distracted by Mom, I locate Nico. He stands there dressed in a dark blue suit with a black shirt and white bow tie. His auburn hair is right at his chin, and his loose waves have me wanting to run my hand through them. My heart flutters, seeming to beat for him in that moment. God. Every time I see him, I swear I start to feel more and more for him.

Scanning me up and down, Nico's eyes halt on my stomach before they shoot back up to mine and he smiles. "You look beautiful."

I don't feel it, but I can't help appreciating what he says. From the box he's holding, he takes out a corsage and places it around my wrist. The flower is blue and white and matches perfectly with my dress. "I love it," I murmur.

"He asked me what color he should get, and I told him the colors of your dress," Mom says as she snaps another photograph. The huge flash on her camera has practically made me dizzy. When my eyes return to normal, she takes another one.

Then comes the cell phone, and Mom takes each picture from every angle imaginable to capture the right photograph. That's what she says, anyway.

"Mom, I think we're about finished here. I don't want us to miss prom." I tug on Nico's arm, pulling him away from Mom's photoshoot.

"One more." She snaps a picture and starts to put it away, but then takes another. "Okay, now I'm finished."

We start to make way for the door. "Nico, have her home in the morning." Then she looks at us with a serious expression. "I know you aren't going to have much of a prom next year, and I know you two won't be getting into trouble since May can't drink with her being pregnant. Go have a good time before you can't put yourselves first anymore."

I can't believe Mom is going to let me stay out all night.

Mom pulls out the index finger, pointing it toward the ceiling. "But. Only this one night."

I run up and hug Mom. I know she's still so disappointed, but she does still love me.

We walk outside to Nico's car, and he opens the door for me. "Are you ready for this?" he asks as he takes his seat in the car.

"No, not really." I laugh.

I've never been into dances, and the only thing I was excited about was the dressing up part. Now that that's over with, I'm not sure.

"Yeah, me neither. We can stay however long and then go wherever you want to."

"Sounds good."

We arrive at the dance and take pictures. I don't know anyone at this school besides Lanie. I spot her, wearing a glistening short pink dress and her hair in loose curls. We walk over to her and chat for a few minutes as a familiar song plays in the background.

There are people everywhere, loads of decorations, and terrible music.

Lanie is with a guy that's a little shorter than me, so I have to look down when I talk to him. He seems nice, and they look like they're really into each other.

We aren't here for very long when Nico leans forward and shouts over the loud music in my ear. "Do you want to get out of here?"

I nod furiously and laugh. "You completely read my mind."

Nico grins and wraps his arm around my shoulders, tugging me to his side. He then steers me out from the dance and away from the shitty music. I could almost kiss him right then.

Once back in the car, I say, "Well, that was a waste of money."

He shakes his head. "No way! I was with you. It was more

than worth it." If he didn't already have my heart, he would from that one simple sentence.

"If you want to go to the parties or something, you can take me home and go. I don't mind." I don't want to spoil his senior prom.

Nico's eyes bulge at me like I've lost my mind. "Are you crazy? This is our night, and we are going to own it."

"That sounds like a phrase from a movie. Better yet, we can make it into a movie. Pregnant girl goes crazy on prom night." I wave my hand like I'm tracing a banner with the words etched in.

Nico chuckles deeply. "Ice cream?"

"Yes! Even better. Pregnant girl eats ice cream on prom night. But, yes, I could go for some ice cream right now." Anytime actually.

Nico drives us to the ice cream shop. We're the only two people who have ventured from the prom to eat ice cream, instead of making our way to the beach for all the house parties.

I order two scoops of vanilla—the soft serve kind.

Nico bumps my shoulder with his. "How boring can you get?" He orders two of the fancier flavors that are mixed with all kinds of fruit and nuts.

"Not boring, but classic."

"Classic is just another term for boring," he says drily.

"Whatever. You're the one who eats hamburgers and sandwiches with only meat and bread. Who else does that besides you?" I give his shoulder a small shove.

He thinks on it for a moment. "I would call that simple."

I roll my eyes. "Simple is the same as boring."

He releases a rumble of laughter, and we find a seat. I finish my ice cream before he's even halfway through with his. I guess I have been getting hungrier lately.

Afterward, we stop by the park and migrate to the swings, talking and swinging like we have no care at all—when we both know we do.

We end up going to Nico's house to find out his parents are already asleep, but Violet is sitting on the couch watching TV with her phone in her hand.

"Aww. My children are back so soon?" she coos, running a hand through her short purple hair. "I thought I wouldn't see you two until tomorrow."

"Oh, you know how it is, sis."

Lowering her eyes to my stomach, Violet leaps over the couch toward me. "You know I don't totally approve of this, but I'm not a parent here—I'm an aunt and going to be a cool one at that." She rubs my stomach which is awkward, but at least she isn't a stranger.

"Before this gets any weirder, we're going to go to my room now." Nico pulls me away, and I follow him down the hall.

Nico changes out of his tux and into a pair of shorts and T-shirt. He picks up his guitar, and I watch him strum on it for a little while. Then we lie on the bed and watch a movie together.

Nico pulls me close to him, and I turn over and start kissing him, his tongue entangling with mine, my tongue dancing with his. We take and we give, kissing for a long time, until the tiredness hits us both. I roll on my side, and he moves closer, pressing his body against mine, enveloping me in his warmth.

"May?"

I turn my head to look at his face. "Yeah?"

He gazes at me like he has something important to say, but then he whispers, "Goodnight."

I want to tell him that I love him, but then I change my mind and reply back with "goodnight," and we both fall asleep.

# Chapter Sixteen

♡

"*I* don't know how long it's been, Mom. I haven't felt the baby move in a long time." I normally feel the baby kick throughout the day. I'm only five and half months pregnant—the baby should be kicking.

"Sometimes you don't feel them all the time, sweetheart." Mom doesn't seem worried when she walks over to press a hand on my stomach and then releases it, like that's magically going to make the baby kick on contact.

Everything about this pregnancy has gone smoothly, except the one day of morning sickness I had. I'd woken up and felt fine in the morning, but on the way to school, I had to pull over and vomit on the side of the road. That was a whole lot of fun.

"The last time was yesterday." I hold my stomach protectively.

"We can call the doctor and see what they'd like for us to do. It's been so long for me that I can't remember how often I felt you kick." Mom lets out a long breath and reaches for the phone to call the doctor.

I don't want to freak out Nico yet, so I shoot Jessie a text. Her dad tried to stay as long as he could, but they ended up moving over a month ago. Things haven't been the same without her, and school is different without her presence.

Me: I haven't felt the baby move in a couple of days.

Now that I'm five and a half months pregnant, I feel like everyone is looking at me, which they probably are. The teachers were for sure, but school recently let out for summer so I can avoid what they might be thinking. My grades have always been good, and I continued to keep them up—but the baby isn't here yet.

"The person that answered the after-hours phone line is going to have a doctor call us back." Mom sinks down beside me, resting her hand on my knee with a look of comfort on her face.

My phone beeps, and I snatch it up.

Jessie: Call the doctor, NOW.

Me: Mom did. We are waiting for her to call us back.

Jessie: Let me know what you find out!!!

Earlier this morning, everything had been great—I wasn't thinking about the kicking. Nico stopped by the house with a surprise for me after sending a text.

*Nico: Meet me outside.*

*Me: What's the occasion?*

*Nico: A surprise.*

*I walked outside, still wearing my pajamas and my hair a full-blown rat's nest, rubbing my hands together in anticipation to see what was inside. He popped open the trunk for me and pulled me around.*

*"Diapers?" One of my eyebrows shot downward. This was the surprise? The trunk had three big boxes of diapers.*

*He propped his hip against the side of his car while he tapped one of the boxes. "I figured if we started getting stuff now, when the time comes, we wouldn't have to buy so much. I know we're going to need a lot, but maybe this will help some."*

*Jetting forward, I threw my arms around his waist. Who would've thought diapers would make me so happy? "I love it."*

I love that he thinks ahead about things I don't even think about.

After about thirty minutes, Mom's phone rings. "Hello." She picks it up and walks with the phone back into the kitchen, tapping a hand against her thigh. She explains what's going on, and there's a lot of her saying "Uh huh."

Rolling off the couch, I follow to where she's standing. I lean in toward the phone so I can listen in. "Okay, I'll bring her right in."

Hanging up the phone, she runs a hand down her cheek. "We're going to the hospital, and they're going to do an ultrasound to make sure everything is fine. It'll also help you feel better when you know the baby is okay." She rubs my shoulder while bobbing her head up and down.

I nod, even though I'm still filled with worry beyond belief.

After Mom grabs her things, I follow her out of the house, and we climb into the car. It feels like forever before we get to the hospital with each second seeming like eons have gone by. I constantly rub my clammy palms together back and forth to keep my hands busy. As soon as I stop moving my hands, I start to feel nervous again.

We arrive at the hospital and are taken immediately to a room. The ride to the second floor in the elevator feels like it takes days. When we get into the room, the nurse straps a baby heart monitor around my stomach to locate the pulse. It feels tight, and I'm patiently waiting to hear the sound, but nothing comes. My chest tightens and panic courses through me, but the nurse doesn't say anything. She removes the heart monitor and walks out of the room, so all I'm left with is the echo of her squeaky sneakers and my rushed thoughts. This is the same hospital where my dad was taken to, and I need better results than he had.

I know Mom wants to run after the nurse and ask her a million questions because of the frown she now has on her face.

"Mom, what's going on?" I murmur, squeezing the edge of the sheet in my hand.

Mom's face is full of question marks, like she isn't sure. "I don't know, sweetheart."

When the nurse comes back into the room, I lay my head against the pillow. Mom stands up out of her chair and pretty much tackles her. "What's going on? Why did you stop using the heart monitor?"

The nurse's expression is blank. "We're sending her down for an ultrasound because I wasn't able to pick up a reading with the heart monitor."

"What does that mean?" I ask, nervously.

"We'll have to wait and see." I know nurses are only doing their job, but most of them I've encountered seem to do their work with a mechanical routine. I know they're probably shutting off their emotions, but it doesn't help the patients.

Another worker, a tall guy with a buzz-cut, rolls in a wheelchair. "Ready for a ride?" he asks.

Staggering out of bed, I move to the wheelchair. "You know I can walk, right?"

"Less work for you." He smiles.

I sit on the pleather seat of the wheelchair, and he pushes me down the white hallway. The hairs on my arms rise due to the coldness of the hospital, and the same over-cleaned smell lingers.

When I'm dropped off at the ultrasound room with Mom, a middle-aged woman tech with black hair and glasses helps lead me to lie down on the table. She pours the cold gel onto my stomach, and I suck in a sharp breath at the ice cube feel of it. Taking hold of the ultrasound stick, she glides it gently across my stomach while watching the screen.

Suddenly her hand stalls, but she finishes up the ultrasound.

"Do you know the results?" Mom asks, impatiently.

"You have to wait for the doctor, but he should be in shortly," she says.

Even though I have to wait for the doctor to tell me what's going on, I know something is seriously wrong here. I know what I already knew, that the baby is gone.

I sit in silence with Mom until the doctor walks into the

room. My worst nightmare is now verified, and I need to decide what to do. I can wait a few hours or wait a few weeks for the natural process to kick in—when my body realizes it isn't carrying a living thing inside me anymore. I can't do that. There's no way I can go several weeks or even one day knowing the baby inside me isn't alive anymore.

The whole idea of being pregnant had been a burden until I felt that first kick. My mind instantly changed, and I started to love the little jelly bean. Nico would play different instruments for the baby, but mostly it would be the guitar, saying the baby's movement got more excited when there was music involved.

Sometimes he would sit headphones on my stomach to give variety. He didn't only do this when I started to show, but even a few weeks after he found out I was pregnant, telling me the baby needed to understand good music at an early age. I guess if early age was considered a tiny bean, then okay.

When we make it back to the room, I find my phone to call Nico. I'm sobbing uncontrollably, and Mom is trying to calm me, but I don't want it.

Blurrily, I scroll to his name and call, and he answers after the second ring. "Hey, I was just about to send you a text. Great minds think alike."

"Nico, I'm at the hospital. Can you please come right away?" I sob.

"May? What's going on?" Worry surrounds every syllable.

I rattle off the hospital and room number and tell him I'll explain when he gets here.

I don't want him to panic and have a wreck from the

emotions he'll be feeling on the way over here. I think he knows, though. I was crying like crazy and still am.

I don't know how much time has passed, but the door opens and Nico hesitantly stands in the entranceway. "May?" he says softly.

Mom steps into the hallway to let me explain to him. Pulling my hands up toward my face, I cry like there's no tomorrow. "Nico, the baby isn't alive anymore."

"What do you mean?" His gaze shifts down to my stomach like he doesn't believe what he heard because my belly still has a baby inside. Then his eyes grow glassy, and he wipes at them with his inner elbow. Walking quickly to the bed, he sits beside me and hauls me up against him, while I sob more tears into his shoulder.

After maybe several hours have gone by, I don't even know because time means nothing to me right now, nurses and staff prep me to be induced.

Nico and my mom are with me while I'm induced. Mom called Nico's parents, and they're waiting out in the lobby with Violet. His parents and Violet have been good to me throughout the pregnancy, but I don't want to see them.

The process is hard and overwhelming—my sweat and tears mixing—and the baby finally comes out. I grip Nico's hand like he's my personal savior and don't let go of it once. It's a girl. No wails, no movement, and no happy smiles from anyone.

A mask covers the bottom portion of the doctor's face, so I'm unable to read his expression. "You have the option to hold the baby if you want to before she's taken away."

I glance back and forth between Mom and Nico, both full

of melancholy.

"I want to hold her," I murmur. I don't want to not know what she would've looked like. A young nurse places the baby in my arms. She's so tiny, already having a hint of auburn fuzz that runs along her scalp. Staring at her closed eyes, I would never think this baby's life is already gone—she's a replica of a sleeping doll.

"Goodbye, Ruby," I whisper. Hot tears slide down my face, and I hand her to Nico. Her last name was going to be Evitts, instead of Falkner.

Nico holds onto her as if she's his entire world. My heart empties until the nurse takes Ruby away, and then my heart is a harness of nothing, a deflated balloon, and a place of loss.

First Dad, then Jessie, and now Ruby. What's next? Who's next?

♥

We have a small funeral for Ruby. I thought about having her cremated, but I wanted a place where I felt like I could go to visit her one day. Mom got a burial spot close to Dad's grave, and Nico's parents insisted on paying for the spot, even though Mom is making more money now from her raise. This time Mom has been the strong one. She's cried, but has really given me support, when none of this would've happened if I hadn't been so stupid and gotten pregnant.

When I get home after the funeral, I become angrier and angrier. I'm still sad, but I'm also frustrated about how suddenly, without any complications, an innocent baby can pass away for no reason. I didn't drink or do drugs. Hell, I even ate healthy, which I didn't do before. I thought I was the master of overcoming death after my dad, but not with this. Not this time.

Over the next week, I do nothing except stay in bed or on the couch. The doorbell rings, and I ignore it. It rings again, so I drag my feet to answer the front door. Nico is standing on the porch looking visibly upset. I haven't talked to him in days and have been avoiding every single one of his texts. I don't know why. I just don't want to see him or anyone.

Leaving the door open, I walk away. "Are you okay, May? I know you aren't okay, but why aren't you talking to me?" he pleads as he closes the door and follows me inside.

I can't even look at his face or his perfect auburn hair, because all I'll see now is Ruby's hair. I whip around quicker than a flash of light and get straight up in his face. "I don't want to talk to you, okay?"

He's straining on what he wants to say. "But, why? I've been there this whole time."

Sighing, I take a few steps back from him. "I know you have, Nico. But I can't look at you anymore. All I see is her face, and I can't think about that right now. I can't think about anything!" My hands fly to my head, and I press on each side like I'm about to crush the thoughts to ashes.

Nico reaches for my arm, and I rip it away. He stands there, lips parted, like I've shot an arrow through his chest, and maybe I have. "She looked like you, too, but I'm not avoiding you." His voice is low and pissed, his gaze turning sharp.

I can't look at him, so I turn around and walk away. "I don't want to see you anymore."

He reaches for my arm again and this time holds onto it to

stop me from walking farther away. "Well, you kind of have to. We still work together," he points out.

I halt and stare him straight in the eye. "No. We don't. I called Violet today and told her I had to quit." There's no way I can go back to work after this and pretend like life is fine.

Gently, his other hand reaches out to touch my face and turns it toward his. "Please don't quit on me, May." His voice is pleading, but his expression pleads even more.

As much as I hate to do it, I can't stay with him. I'm too angry, too upset, too crazy to go on and pretend everything is fine. I'd spiral out of control and make him hate me, which I'm probably doing right now. So, why does it matter?

"We're done here, and I want you to leave. I don't want to see you or your face again." Ripping my arm out of his hand, I shove at his chest to get out.

I head toward the door, yanking it open and step back a few feet to where he's still standing. "Leave. Forget about me, and forget I ever existed. That's what I'm about to do to you."

"You can't erase people," he spits out.

"This is all your damn fault!" I yell.

I don't know why I'm blaming him. We both know we share the fault, but at this moment, I don't care. I want *him* gone. I want *everyone* gone.

He clenches his teeth. "Whatever. I'm not going to stand around and listen to this shit. If you ever need me, call me."

"Don't hold your breath. You're nothing to me and never have been, so stay the fuck away from me." I clench my tongue between my teeth to avoid telling him I don't mean it.

Angrily, he turns and walks away with steam practically radiating from his shoulders. He slams the door in my face, and I fall to the floor, curling up into a tight ball. I hate everything. I hate myself more than anything.

I fall into a spiral of depression and can barely talk to anyone for the rest of the summer. The hospital performed tests for the baby's cause of death, and the results came back that there was nothing wrong. When senior year starts back up, I dive into schoolwork and focus only on that. Any other outside activity, I avoid. I come home, finish my schoolwork and plunge into art for hours upon hours until it's time for bed. Then I continue this endless routine over and over and over.

Mom can't handle it, and she takes me to her counselor who she saw after Dad died. I tell her repeatedly I don't need the counseling, and unlike after Dad died, she knew I needed it this time.

The counseling doesn't help at first until around the end of my senior year. Finally, it starts to open my chest back up like a blooming flower—emotions pour out, and I'm sorry. Sorry about everything. Sorry about Dad and Ruby, and sorry I didn't let Nico help me get through it all.

It's too late for Nico and me, but I have my phone in my hand, ready to send him a text. I had deleted his number, but I still remember it, locked away in my brain like a precious treasure waiting to be found.

I can't do it. Not only because I yelled horrible things at him, but I don't want to be a reminder to him, either. Too much time has passed, it isn't like it has been a week since I last talked to him. It has almost been an entire year, so I set my phone down and hope he finds happiness somewhere else.

# *Chapter Seventeen*

$\heartsuit$

Two years have gone by since I last talked to Nico, and I still miss him more than I can explain. Two years have passed since I lost Ruby, and I wish I could've known her. I've managed to mend my friendship with Jessie after completely cutting her off when I lost Ruby. I'm still mad at myself for doing that. She never gave up on me, though. She constantly bugged me with texts and emails, until one day I responded, and all she said was that it was about time.

Mom found me a part-time job at her work doing data entry. I'm saving up enough money, so that next year when I attend the university, I'll have enough for an apartment. I want to try living on my own for a while.

For the past year, I've been going to the cemetery at least once a month. Today, I'm going to visit Dad and Ruby there. I think it's finally time to do the headstone rubbings on both of their markers.


Me: You're missing out on some headstone rubbings today.

Jessie: I swear when I finish college and get a real job, I'll fly there, and we can go across the state looking for new cemeteries.

Me: I'm down for that.

Jessie: Are you feeling okay today?

Me: I feel better than last year, and the year before that, so it's a pretty good start.

Jessie: Send me the pictures when you're finished. I want to show Henry.

Henry is Jessie's boyfriend, and they have been dating for about five months. He seems like a decent guy, and I'm so happy for her. I always thought she'd never get past the loser phase, but she did. If anyone has grown into a more mature person, it's Jessie.

Gathering my supplies, I throw them in a bag for the cemetery, adding the new pack of wax crayons I bought yesterday.

I snatch the bag and pack a lunch in the kitchen, finding Mom sitting at the table already eating. "Hey, Sweetie."

"Hey, Mom." I give her a small smile, walk to the cabinet and locate the bread that has been sitting in the pantry for a week. Sometimes I feel bad about the bread. I forget it's there, and then by the time I reach for it, it's already old and moldy—it could've been fed to someone else. Maybe I'll bring the rest of the bread to feed the birds that are sometimes at the pond by the graveyard.

Mom sets her spoon down, making a clinking sound against her soup bowl. "Do you want me to go with you today?"

Any other day I wouldn't mind, but today I kind of want alone time. "How about next time?"

Picking up a napkin, she dabs at her mouth. "Any time you need me to go, I don't mind." I know she knows I'm a lot better, but she continues to be concerned.

"I know." Mom has become different these past two years. She seems stronger and more independent. I know she still misses Dad at times, but she has also managed to live without him. She isn't quite ready to date, and I'm not sure if she ever will be, but either way, I'm fine with her decision.

For me, I don't think I could marry again after what she went through and being married for so long. But I haven't been in her situation, so I don't know.

There's a guy at work who has creepily been hitting on Mom, and it's directly in front of me. I don't think she quite gets it, and when I tell her, she says he's only being nice. Yeah … nicely always touching her arm.

After I finish making my sandwich, I tell Mom goodbye and head out the front door. It feels hot and muggy, and I should probably have worn a pair of shorts instead of pants.

Tossing everything in the backseat of my car, I make sure the bread I grabbed on the way out is sitting on top in pristine condition. *Give it up, May. I don't think the birds care if their bread is mushed or nice and fluffy. Am I becoming one of those bird ladies now? Oh, my god, I am, aren't I? A freaking nineteen-year-old bird lady!* I slam the door and push that horrendous thought aside, sending Jessie one last quick text before I leave.

Me: I have officially become a bird lady.

On the way to the cemetery, I'm stuck in traffic. I have the window rolled up with my own personal concert blasting its way to my ears. In no way, shape or form am I a singer, but right here and right now, I'm performing a live concert. My singing is terrible, but it has me feeling good.

When I arrive at the cemetery, I have to sit in the car for a few minutes to get myself ready. I thought I was prepared, but in actuality, I may only be two-thirds prepared.

I breathe in and out a total of three times. For some reason, I have the palm of my hand facing me and moving with me when I breathe in, and then I face my palm out when I breathe out. Now, I'm turning into Mom—she always does that.

Shaking my head, I step out of the car and take everything from the back. There are a few cars in the parking lot, but I don't look at them.

The clouds are out in full force today, like Dad is saying "hello."

"Hey, Dad," I whisper as I gaze toward the clouds.

I walk through the cemetery and stare straight ahead, that's when I freeze. Quickly, I duck down behind a headstone.

"You know I can see you over there, May."

"Shit," I hiss. Did I just curse in the cemetery? Is that forbidden or something? Looking at the headstone I ducked behind, I can see it's probably only covering about one-fourth of my entire body.

Slowly, I peep around the corner and see a bright purple head, and she's grinning at me. "Did you think that little headstone could cover your gigantic body?" Violet has her arms crossed over her chest.

I stand up like I have no idea what she's talking about. "Maybe?"

I look all around to see if Nico is with her. What would I

do if he was here? Probably try and hide behind the headstone again.

"He isn't here," Violet says, walking toward me.

"Oh. I'm not sure what you're talking about." I glance past her at the pond, as if I'm busy somehow.

Violet lets out a chuckle. "Sure, you don't."

She stops in front of me, and I realize how much I've missed her. "It's been a long time. I brought some bread. Do you want to feed the birds?" I pull open the full loaf of bread like it's my prized possession.

Violet stares at the bread like I've lost my mind. "Um. Okay."

She follows me when I trek to the pond, and I set everything on the ground except for the bread.

"So, how have you been?" I ask.

I hand Violet a piece of bread, and she pitches it into the water like she's a softball player. "I'm leaving for New York tomorrow. I got a job at a gallery up there, and they're offering to hang some of my stuff as well."

Fishing out a slice for myself, I throw it to the edge of the pond where several crows fly down and peck at it piece by piece. "That's so awesome. I knew your work would go somewhere someday." Her art is too good for her to stick around here.

"Not to sound cocky, but I knew it would, too." She throws another piece harder this time.

I let out a laugh. "So, I guess you won't be managing the bookstore anymore."

She's about to throw another piece of bread and stops. "No. The one who shall not be named is going to be in charge for now." She looks at me straight in the eye, probably trying to gauge my reaction.

My heart temporarily freezes and I nod, letting no reaction cross my face. "What are you doing here today?" I change the subject because I can't talk about Nico, especially with her— it would hurt too much.

Violet stares down at her toes like she's not sure what to say. "I wanted to visit Ruby before I left. I know I don't come here much. I don't know why it is, but it's still hard to think about."

A tear slowly streams down my face that I had no idea had taken form. I wipe it away with my hand in a fist. "I know. It took me a long time to get where I'm at right now." I still think about Ruby all the time, wondering what stage of life she would be at now and what she would've looked like.

Lifting her head, she looks me directly in the eyes with sorrow filling hers. "I hate myself for acting like it's hard to think about when you're the one who went through it. I was only on the sideline."

Violet shifts from one foot to the other. "I want you to know I would've been there for you and Ruby. I never got to tell you that."

The tears are now dropping full blast, and Violet has tears streaming down her face, too. I've never seen her sad the whole time I have known her. "I know. You told me you'd have helped with babysitting and all that."

"Well, I want to make sure you know."

"I know." And I do.

After the bread is gone, we walk to Ruby's headstone. I wanted to come alone, but I'm happy Violet is here with me.

It isn't uncomfortable, it's comforting. Taking out my lunch, I hand Violet half my sandwich. We sit down on the grass and talk for a while, mainly about what she's going to do once she leaves and how school is going for me. She doesn't once mention Nico, and I don't ask about him either.

When we finish eating, she stands up to leave, but then kneels back down in front of me—her expression is serious. "You know my number is still the same if you ever need me."

"I won't be bothering you in New York! I do want to see some of that famous artwork one day, though."

Violet laughs. "Don't worry, it will be sooner than you think."

We both move to stand, and she gives me one of her lightning-fast hugs before turning to walk away.

"Hey, Violet," I call.

"Yeah?"

"Can you not tell him you saw me?" I don't want to mess up his life any more than I did.

She lets out a sigh that tells me she wants to argue, then she holds up her index finger. "Only this once, but if I run into you anywhere again, I'm telling him. Got it?"

I give her a sad smile. "Fine." I doubt I'll be running into her since she's moving to New York.

Violet gives me one last wave, and I watch her purple head all the way to her car.

I put away my lunch trash and work on Ruby's headstone rubbing, making hers multi-colored while talking to her as I work.

"You know, Ruby, things would've been hard for a while with me in school, but we would've made it work. Your dad, he would've been the one always keeping it all in check. I think there would've been a lot of hard times once you were here, but there would've been a whole lot of good times, too." I tear up a little, but I'm okay, and I continue talking to her.

When her rubbing is complete, I admire all the different colors that resemble a rainbow, reminding me that once the rain has cleared, something beautiful can always appear. I roll it up gently and place it in a tube. I want to keep this one forever. It may seem weird that I want to keep a headstone rubbing, but it feels like more than that. It'll remind me of this day with her, and how I felt okay.

Next, I grab my things off the ground and walk to Dad's headstone. Kneeling in front of the grave marker, I rest my hand on top. "I know you've been watching over Ruby. Thanks for that. I want you to know Mom has been a lot better. She still misses you more than anything, but she's okay."

I sit there for a few minutes before I pull out another sheet of paper and begin on his with different shades of blues. Blue was his favorite color, but it always changed. One day it may have been a sky blue. Then another day it was midnight blue, but it was always blue.

After I finish up Dad's, I roll up the paper and place it in a separate tube. I pack up all my things and get ready to head home, taking one last look at the cemetery. Blowing out a breath, I give this place, meant for so much sadness, a smile. I can't help but feel like maybe there's something for me to do in this life one day. I'm not completely ready, but I'm getting there.

# Chapter Eighteen

♡

*7* finish packing up my last box and throw it in the back of my trunk, wondering how Violet's art is doing in New York. I haven't seen her since a year ago at the cemetery.

When Mom and I got back from my new apartment, we packed and moved the last of everything ourselves without movers. Not that I had *that* much.

I bought a futon for the living room and put that together myself, luckily. Mom had no earthly idea what was going on with that contraption.

"Are you sure you want to move out and not stay here until you're finished with college?" Mom asks.

I close the lid of the trunk. "I need this, and anytime you need me, I can come right on over."

Living with Mom isn't that bad, but when I already work with her during the week, it can be exhausting. I've been saving most of my money since Mom hasn't made me pay any bills, except the car insurance and cell phone. I offered to help out more, but she wasn't having it. She said I could worry about that after college.

"You're only twenty. Can't you wait a little longer?" She has her hands on her hips with her lips in a pout.

"Jessie moved out as soon as she finished high school, so I feel like I'm a little behind."

Mom shakes her head, probably still wishing I was eight years old. "Okay, but give me a call tonight after you've settled in." She gives me a long hug, and I have to wiggle myself out of it.

"Talk to you soon. I love you, Mom." I wave and hop in the car to head for the apartment. I don't know how long I'm going to stay at the job with Mom, because I'm going to start subbing in the fall for the school district to get some teaching experience under my belt.

Pulling up to the apartment, I pop open the trunk. I had laid the seats forward and practically threw my whole closet in the backseat. Collecting as many clothes on hangers as I can, I toss them over my arm and head for my apartment door.

The keys are in my hand, and I'm trying to fiddle with them to get in position to open the door, but they make a clinking sound as they hit the ground. I struggle to try and pick them up without spilling all my clothes across the cement. *Why didn't I unlock the door first?* I pick up the keys and get them in the knob. Success! The door is now unlocked.

Strolling into my apartment, I drop the first load of clothes on the bed and will worry about hanging them up later. I repeat the process of lugging stuff from my car several times. Maybe I should've donated a lot of these clothes.

By the time I head down for the last items, my mouth is dry, and the back of my shirt clings to my skin. I slam the trunk shut and grab the last small box of my things from the front seat.

Shutting the door, I quickly move forward without looking

for anyone around. Big mistake. I hit a person, and the box I'm holding tumbles downward, but I catch it at the last second.

"Sorry," I say. "I should've looked where I was going before I started moving." I notice the black hair that's cut in a short bob, but I don't even pay attention to the face.

"May?" a soft voice asks. I now focus on her face, and it takes me a second to recognize it with the different hair.

"Lanie? What are you doing here?" I haven't seen her in years and had only been around her a handful of times. This is weird.

She brushes a lock of hair behind her ear. "I live here, or I did live here. I'm moving in with my boyfriend."

"I thought you were going to college out of state." I adjust the box in my hands while glancing at my open, apartment door, hoping nothing strange crawls in.

"I was, but I decided to stay local to be close to my family."

"Okay, well it was good seeing you. I've got to get this box inside." I don't need this conversation to start getting into any sort of awkward territory.

Turning around, she stares at my door, and her eyes widen. "You're living there?"

"Uh. Yeah?" Is this apartment haunted or something?

A small smile spreads across her face. "You know—"

I don't even notice the other person running over, but I hear the guy's voice. "Lanie, you forgot your phone."

Lanie turns around, and her small smile turns into a full-on glowing one. I look at the other person who has stopped in his place. My heart freezes at the sight of him before speeding up, so fast that I think my rib cage may crack. His auburn hair is a lot shorter than it used to be but still has some length on top.

Nico looks good. Better than good.

I glance between the two, and I'm not sure what to do. "Okay, well, it was good seeing you, Lanie." I dart past her, nodding in Nico's direction with a weird head tilt. "Nico." Then I haul butt inside the apartment and close the door. I bolt all the locks behind me and set the box on the floor. Do I think one of them is going to come in and try to rob me?

What do I do next? I peer out the peephole of course. Nico is just standing there. What is he doing here? My heart's pounding grows even stronger. Lanie is talking away to him, then she points in my direction. I move away from the door, afraid they can see me through the tiny hole—I'm finished trying to be a spy.

I tiptoe toward my room, but who am I kidding? Running back to the peephole, I peer out again. Nico's hands are moving back and forth, and Lanie keeps pointing at my door. Are they together? Does she think something is going on between Nico and me? No, that can't be it. She said she had a boyfriend. Oh, maybe Nico is her boyfriend? Shit.

Leaving the door, I inspect the kitchen to see what there is to eat to distract myself and block out all things Nico. Oh, yeah. I have nothing. I need to go shopping.

I do have a whole pack of bottled water and a big tub of cheese balls, though. This will have to be sufficient for my needs right now. I unscrew the cap of the cheese balls when there's a loud knock at the door.

I startle and scream, and the cheese balls fly everywhere. All over the counter, sprawled across the floor—I think one even went down my shirt.

Should I answer the door? No, I think I'm going to stay right here and admire all the cheese balls everywhere. Maybe I can even take a picture and make it into some weird artsy photograph. What the hell am I even talking about?

As I walk toward the door, another knock sounds. Slowly, I check out the peephole and see an auburn head turned away from the door. Okay, let's be cool here. I'm an adult now. We're both adults. We can talk about things like adults. Can't we? But what do I even say?

My hand shakes as it unlocks each lock, including the chain at the top, and I pull the door open but not all the way.

Startled, Nico spins around. Did he think I wasn't home and magically vanished? I know he saw me come in here.

"Hey," he says. There's no sign of a smile on his face anywhere. His mouth is closed with his lips pressed into a thin line.

"Hey," I reply. I'm not smiling either. I'm scared, and I don't know why. "Um. It's been a long time."

Tilting his head to the side, he pops his neck. "You could say that."

I open the door all the way. "Do you want to come in?"

He glances side to side. *What's he looking for?* "Alright."

I've missed him so damn much. I don't know why I didn't at least text him over the past few years—nothing I can do about that now.

"The options are limited at the moment, but I do have a futon. It may or may not be comfortable. I haven't really tried sitting on it yet." I point him in the direction of the futon, and he heads for it. Closing the door behind me, I follow him. It may seem strange, but I want to yank him back and pull him in a long hug, making up for lost time.

He takes a seat, and I hesitate at first but then plop down a few feet away from him. "So, you live here now?" he asks.

"No, I'm just moving all my stuff in and then going somewhere else." I give a weird laugh. *Why did I laugh like that?*

"I see you haven't lost your sense of humor." As he smiles, I want to grab it, place it in my pocket, and carry it around with me. I've missed that smile.

My eyebrows lift up my forehead as I think about something. "What are you doing here?"

"Well, you did invite me in." He tilts his head forward and to the side.

I shake my head. "No, I mean at these apartments."

Looking as if he's going to let me in on a little secret, he inches slightly closer. "I live right next door." He points to the right.

My jaw drops a little. Okay, I wasn't expecting that. At least I don't have to be concerned about having a crappy neighbor, but now I have to worry about having Nico as a neighbor.

"Let me know if I'm ever too loud when I play an instrument, with the walls being paper thin and all."

"Oh." I shrug. "I don't mind. I never minded listening to you play."

He runs his hand across the back of his neck. "Are you going to school here, too?"

Leaning against the back of the couch, I think that this doesn't feel weird at all. It feels like we're old friends reuniting with a long history. No. I'm lying. It's incredibly weird.

"Yeah, I finished up at the community college, but I'm taking some courses here this summer. I'm starting one tomorrow evening."

Nico leans forward with his elbows resting on his jeans. "Oh yeah? Me too. What class are you taking?"

"I needed an extra art-type class, so I wanted to do something laid back for the summer. It's supposed to be some intro to motion pictures course. One of the students in a class I had last semester said it was a breeze. You pretty much watch movies and have quizzes about them." I could've just said the name of the class instead of rambling on.

A shocked expression crosses his face as his lips part. "No shit. That's the same course I'm taking."

I feel like there are way too many coincidences going on today. Well, maybe only two, but they're huge. The class thing isn't that surprising, but out of everywhere and then all the apartments here, Nico happens to be my neighbor.

There isn't going to be much avoiding him, and if I'm honest with myself, I don't think I want to avoid him anymore. Being friends is easy, we never had a problem with that.

Nico checks the screen on his phone. "Sorry to cut this short, but I have to go to work. I'm running late already."

My chest sinks a little at him having to leave, but I don't say anything. "Oh. Okay. You probably need to get back to Lanie."

Standing up from the couch, he places his phone in his pocket. "No. Lanie already left. She's on her way to meet up with her boyfriend."

That settles that question. Lanie's boyfriend isn't Nico. Is it wrong for me to feel good about this? Maybe it is, but I do.

I walk him to the door, and he stands there for a few seconds. "If you need anything, I'm right next door. Let me give you my number just in case."

A small smile tugs at my lips. "I remember it. Do you need mine?"

Smiling back, he says, "I remember it."

"Okay, well, see you tomorrow in class, Nico." I watch him as he starts to walk next door.

Lifting his head, he glances over his shoulder at me. "Likewise, May."

I close the door behind me. "Just friends. I can do it." My chest expands from thinking about this. We have a history that ended pretty badly, but none of it matters right now.

Taking out my phone, I send Jessie a text.


Me: Guess who lives next door?

Jessie: A hot guy?

Me: Nico.

Jessie: What??????????????? Are you okay with it?

Me: Yes.

Jessie: It's starting, isn't it?

Me: No.

But she knows me better than I know myself. She always has.

♥

I'm sitting at work trying not to think about class tonight, or the fact I'll definitely be seeing Nico there when my phone goes off.

Jessie: Guess who got engaged?

Me: What????

I've only heard good things about Henry, so I can't help but be excited for her. I'm a little disappointed I still haven't met him, but I will one day.

She sends a picture of the ring, and a blue sapphire rests in the middle, surrounded by tiny white diamonds embedded in the band. The ring is beautiful.

Me: I'm going to admit I'm a little jealous about that ring!

Not the engagement, though. I'm more shocked she didn't get engaged sooner than this.

Jessie: We're going to wait until after I finish college. So, we'll be planning next year. I know it's far off, but you're going to be my maid of honor!

Me: Am I?

Jessie: Will you?

Me: Duh!

Jessie decided to go the nursing route, and this upcoming year will be her last couple of semesters in the program before she'll be able to officially be a nurse. Nursing was the last career I would've thought she'd have chosen, but she's interested in all aspects of it.

I get back to work until my fingers cramp. Glancing at the clock on the computer, I realize it's a few minutes until lunch. I'm meeting Mom up front, and she's taking me to the deli across the street.

Sandwiches may only be sandwiches to some people, but these are *sandwiches!* Mom's wearing a tight, black, pencil skirt to her knees and a bright green blouse. She has started to dress up more over the past month, and from behind people would probably think she's in her early twenties.

She's been working out a lot lately, and I didn't notice until now how good she looks for her age.

"Hey, sweetheart, I missed you last night," Mom says when she pats my shoulder.

I shake my head. "You'll be fine. So, I got some big news."

Mom holds the door open for me as we step outside. "What news? I'm all ears." She's all about gossip. She may not be a work gossip, but she's like the number one celebrity gossip queen and can tell you who did what, who is dating who, who had whose baby, etc. If only this type of knowledge was useful.

Mom gnaws on her lip, looking anxious. "Real life news, Mom."

"Oh?" she says, her interest piqued, as we cross the street.

"Jessie is engaged!"

Mom practically jumps in the air. "No way. All I see is Jessie as a little kid still. Does she already have a date set?"

We walk into the deli. "No, not yet. She's going to wait until she's finished with school, so it won't be until next year."

"Smart girl."

Stepping to the counter to place my order, I stare at the menu debating, finally settling on a chicken salad sandwich. This is no normal chicken salad sandwich. It's the best one I've ever tasted. I order iced tea to drink, and a small bowl of mixed fruit filled with apples, strawberries, blueberries, and grapes.

Mom has already located a small table, and I sit directly in front of her. "How do you like your apartment?"

"It seems nice so far. Nico is my neighbor." Taking a bite out of my sandwich, I await her reaction.

She starts choking and grabs her bottled water to take a swig. Then she sets the bottle down and gives me a small frown. "Nico?"

I swallow my food. "Yes, as in Nico-Nico. I found out yesterday he's my neighbor, and apparently, he's going to be in my summer class."

"You didn't mention this last night!" she shrieks. Then she tries to hide the fact that she practically yelled and whispers, "Are you okay about this? You two have been through some difficult times in the past."

"When I talked to you last night, it kind of slipped my mind. Yeah, I'm fine with it. Maybe I wouldn't have been fine several years ago, but I am now."

Okay, it didn't really slip my mind, but I didn't want to hear Mom go on about it for hours. I also had to tell her. If she were to run into him when she comes over, that would be a big huge pile of awkward. I know Mom is concerned, but the fact is, I'm okay.

I drink some of my tea when she speaks again. "You do have protection, right?"

I spit out the tea, and it's my turn to cough. "What?"

"Look, I know you aren't a baby anymore, but you're still my baby. I know stuff happens when we least expect it, and something spontaneous may happen when you aren't thinking about it. I want to make sure you're prepared in case something does." She leans a little forward to examine me.

"I don't even know if I'll even be seeing him besides in class, and it isn't like that anyway. If something were ever to happen one day with anyone, I'm on birth control, as you know." My cheeks heat up a little with this discussion, like we're out on a picnic casually talking about this.

She releases a long sigh. "I know you never really wanted to talk to me about how things ended. There was something special between you two, even though you both were so young. You're still young, but you have a good head on your shoulders." I don't know what I'm feeling right now, but I do know we had something good.

We talk a little longer and finish our lunch before we have to head back to the office. It's weird how the relationship between mother and daughter changes over the course of your life, especially with all we have been through together. She's still my mom and will always throw in her two cents, but she has become more than that.

# Chapter Nineteen

$\heartsuit$

The rest of work flies by quickly, and I head home, stopping first by the grocery store. I have a few hours before class begins, so I clean the kitchen and living room. The apartment manager said they cleaned the place up before I moved in, but it still feels like it needs a little TLC.

After I finish cleaning, I eat a quick bite and get ready for class, throwing a spiral notebook and a couple of pens in my backpack along with a few snacks. Then I leave for class.

The parking lot is already full, and I park ridiculously far away from the building. It's okay, though. I don't mind walking. I let out a few breaths before stepping out of the car because I know I'll be seeing Nico.

I haven't been to the campus, so I'm not exactly sure where to go. But I easily find the building. Then I roam around before, finally, locating the room number I need.

Glancing at my phone, I see I'm about ten minutes early, and a few people are already sitting in class. My chest gets that funny feeling when I spot Nico already sitting in a seat with his earbuds in, consumed by a book. Appearing cuter than ever.

I can bet anything that he's listening to classical music—

he always tended to do that. Anytime I read, it has to be in complete silence. I can't read at school, a coffee shop, or anywhere that has the slightest bit of noise.

Walking toward where he's seated, I think to myself that maybe I should sit somewhere else, but I want to mend our friendship. I'm not sure if he wants to, but I want to at least say I tried.

Nico is lost in his own head with his book in one hand, and his other hand playing a symphony against his leg.

Grabbing hold of one of his earbuds, I place it against my ear, and orchestra music, with a slower rhythm, drifts out from the speaker. I'm not good at identifying what instruments they are, but it's classical. "I knew it!"

He gives me a quizzical look. "What?"

Removing my backpack from my shoulders, I plop it down on the floor and take a seat. "I knew you were listening to classical music. Every time I saw you studying or reading, you were always listening to it."

Nico puts the book away and pulls out his one remaining earbud. "I can't help it that the sounds help me concentrate."

I tried it one time when I was at his house studying for a test, and I gave up after about three minutes. All I kept hearing were pulsating knocks, and it wasn't working one bit.

"How was work?" I ask. I'm trying to make conversation.

"I came straight here after I got off—it was alright. Ever since Violet left, I've had to do a lot. She always seemed like she had nothing to do and made it appear so easy." She did make it look effortless. Most of the time she was drawing in the office, but still managed to get everything done.

Leaning over, I unzip my backpack to drag out the

notebook and pen I brought. "I think she was good at multitasking. Either that or she had a little magical person sitting around doing all her work."

"You know, I can see that." He chuckles.

"How is she liking New York?"

Both of his auburn eyebrows shoot upward. "How did you know she moved to New York?"

Crap. Do I lie? Do I tell him the truth? I don't feel like it's a big deal now. "Well, I saw her about a year ago, and she told me about New York."

Nico's lips purse together, his forehead wrinkling from his surprised expression. "She never told me about this."

I'm about to answer when the teacher walks in and saves the day. The class is full, and I somehow missed everyone coming into the room and taking their seats.

The teacher, Mr. Hendricks, passes out the syllabus for the summer session. I catch myself rubbing my hands together in anticipation to see what the movie list is going to be, and I stop doing this strange movement.

Mr. Hendricks looks old. He not only looks old but is old, like in his seventies. He's wearing an old suit, and I'm straining to see what is on his tie. When he gets close enough, I notice the white spots are ducks on his tie. Interesting.

He hands me a green sheet of paper, and I scan through, immediately slouching in my chair.

"Disappointed?" Nico whispers.

"Yes! I've never heard of any of this stuff before," I whisper back.

I know a lot of movies because when I was in junior high, Jessie and I got into a big movie phase. When we took turns spending the weekends at each other's houses, we would do a different theme each month.

We did the eighties, romantic comedies, horror, indies, comic book, you name it. Then when Dad started getting sick and spent most of his weekends at home, we watched more movies. Even if I haven't seen the films, I've usually heard the name—not on this list, though.

Mr. Hendricks walks back up to the front of the room. His voice is pure monotone, and his first few sentences are putting me to sleep. The class does seem easy, and we only meet two nights a week. The first day of the week is the movie. The next day of the week, we turn in a short paper about our thoughts on the film and have a ten-question quiz.

Since the summer session is jam packed into such a small time frame, he's going to start the movie tonight. We have the option of staying here to watch the film, but if we have it or can rent it from somewhere else, we're free to leave.

I plan on going home and ordering it from somewhere to watch—then I can pause it or do whatever.

Nico leans over when I start packing up my stuff. "You aren't going to stay to watch the movie?"

I look at the front of the room toward Mr. Hendricks and back to Nico. "Um, I'm going to have to pass on that. I'm going to sit on my semi-comfortable futon and watch it from there."

"Oh, okay." He nods.

Hesitating for a split second, afraid he'll say no, I ask, "If you want to stay here then more power to you, but you can come over and watch it if you want."

"Are you sure?" He's already putting his stuff away in his

backpack.

"Yes, I'm sure. No one deserves to sit for two hours in these chairs." I laugh while examining the hard seats.

Outside, it's already dark but still hot as hell. "Where did you park?" I ask.

He points to a silver truck in the front row.

"How did you manage to snag that spot? I'm way the crap out there." I point to destination nowhere.

Nico cracks a side smile. "Well, when I got here, I drove down this row, and the spot was empty. So, I took it."

I wish I had that type of luck today. "Smart ass. I'll see you when we get back to the apartment." I turn to leave and only make it two steps before he grabs the top of my backpack and stops me in place.

"I can drive you to your car."

I shake my head. "This is my workout for the day. You don't want to interrupt that, do you?"

Nico releases my backpack and smiles. "Okay, but be careful."

Whipping out my pepper spray that's already in my hand, I drag it up so he can see it up close and personal. "I'm already locked and loaded."

He rolls his eyes toward the night sky. "That you are. Do you need me to pick anything up on the way over?"

"It's your lucky day. I went to the grocery store earlier so there are plenty of snacks and drinks." I grin as I start walking to find my car. "See ya."

I'm secretly excited and nervous that Nico is coming over. The journey through the parking lot is a disaster. Somehow, I forgot where I parked, and I keep clicking the unlock button until I hear a beep and find my car. If only I had a bright green car—black blends in everywhere I go.

When I get home, Nico is already parked in the parking lot, and I pull into the empty space beside him.

He steps out of his truck at the same time I get out of my car. "Took you long enough," he says.

I yank my bag from the floor on the passenger side—it rolled off the seat earlier. "We can't all have VIP parking at the school."

Nico comes up beside me, his intoxicating, soapy scent hitting my nose. "So, where are you working now?"

"I've been at the office where my mom works for a while—I do a lot of data entry. It's basically typing all day long, but I only work there three days a week. I'm going to start subbing in the fall and working around my school schedule."

"That sounds interesting. How's your mom?"

I laugh because I know data entry does not sound interesting. "Interesting is code word for boring, and yes, it's extremely boring. She's doing good—she's been getting into a lot of different hobbies. Some are a win, and some are a loss."

Once inside, I grab a packaged cookie and offer Nico one, which he more than happily accepts. I walk to the TV and search on my phone to try and locate the movie from the list. It's some super old war movie, and it's two and a half hours long. I manage to find it and click the rent button.

"What's the deal with all these cheese balls?"

"Huh?" Turning around, I look at Nico whose hand is hovering over the trash can to throw away his wrapper.

*Oh. Those cheese balls.* The ones I spilled all over the kitchen when he was at the door. I guess he didn't notice them everywhere when he came in the day before. "I dropped the container yesterday, and those little morsels didn't make it into my intestines."

He takes a seat beside me on the futon. "You know, I'm kind of surprised you didn't bottle them back up and eat them. I remember how much you love cheese balls."

I set the remote down. "I'm going to be honest here. I did think about it, but then I don't know who lived here before me, who walked in the kitchen, what crawled in the kitchen, so I had to pass on that."

Leaning back against the futon, Nico stares at the TV. "You're still the same."

He's right and wrong about that. I still have my same quirks, but I think about things in life a lot differently.

Loading the movie on the TV, I then stand up to grab juice boxes from the fridge for Nico and me—also snatching a bag of chips for him. I'm not that hungry, so I sip on my box and start the movie. It's nice sitting here next to him, and it feels like old times. A rush of good memories stirs inside me, and my heart swells. But for now, I push them away.

The movie has to be one of the worst war movies I've ever seen. Maybe I'm not the movie pro I thought I was because I've never considered the war movie genre. It has to be the one genre I stayed away from.

I take a glance at Nico who looks to be struggling about as much as I am. My eyes keep straining to stay open, and at some point during the movie, I drift off to sleep.

# *Chapter Twenty*

♡

*I* wake up latched onto Nico, feeling super comfortable, warm.

My arms are strapped around him like he's a big stuffed teddy bear, and my knees curled up to my stomach.

Lifting my head, I look at poor Nico, who is still sitting with his feet flat on the floor, but his upper body is tilted all the way down on his side.

My eyes drift to the TV that's still on, and I shake Nico awake. "Hey, you fell asleep."

His eyes flutter open for a second—then he smiles and drifts back to sleep. "Nico," I sing terribly to try and wake him.

Ugh, he's still hard to wake up, and I don't know if he has work or anything today. I'm off, so it doesn't matter what time I would've slept until.

He doesn't budge, so I grab his arm and continuously move it back and forth to wake him. "Nico!" I shout.

That does the trick. He pulls himself to a sitting position and massages his lower back, seeming like he may have a cramp there. "What time is it?" he asks groggily.

I glance at the clock. "It's seven-forty. I wasn't sure if you have work today."

His eyes half close and then reopen, looking like he's

ready to lie right back down in the uncomfortable position and go back to sleep. "I don't have to be in until ten today, but I do have to take a shower."

"Do you want me to make you something to eat first? I'm starving." I get off the couch and hover over him.

"You know how to cook these days?" He glances over at the kitchen in surprise.

I pucker my lips out. "I haven't made it that far in life yet, but I'll get there one day. Eggs?"

"Sure. Can I use your bathroom?" He rises from the couch and attempts to pop his back.

"Yeah, it's right down the hall." I point in the direction of the bathroom.

Heading into the kitchen, I pull out my one frying pan and then take out the carton of eggs. I throw a couple onto the pan and pop a couple pieces of toast in the toaster, and I feel like a professional chef.

For years Mom has been offering to teach me her cooking skills, and I'm going to take her up on that offer soon.

I turn around and startle when I see Nico already sitting at the counter. "Geez! I didn't even hear or see you come back."

"You looked too entranced by those eggs." He nods at them. "By the way, I think they're burning."

"Shit." I hurry and turn off the stove top and pour some of the eggs onto a plate for him and then for me. They may be a little burnt but still edible.

I must have missed the two pieces of toast popping up because there they are on full display ready to be plucked. Grabbing the two plates with eggs, I set a piece of toast on each plate and pour two glasses of juice. I get us each a fork, and I'm *done*. Oh yeah, that's why I don't want to cook, it's tiring.

He's already stuffing eggs in his mouth. "How is it?" I ask.

"These are the worst eggs I've ever eaten." He smiles.

"Damn." I laugh.

"I'm just kidding. They taste good." He lifts his orange juice and takes a swallow. "On to other things. What was this about Violet?"

I thought maybe he had forgotten that whole situation, but I guess he hasn't.

After a few seconds pass, I sigh. "I ran into her about a year ago at the cemetery. We talked for a while, and she told me about New York."

"She must have let that slip her mind," he mumbles.

I stare at my plate of food. "To be fair, I told her not to tell you. I didn't want to interrupt your life."

He lays the fork down on his plate. "You never would've interrupted my life, May. Do you know how much I've missed you this entire time?" I've missed him, too, but then I think about seeing Lanie the other day.

"I don't know. You seemed pretty comfortable having Lanie for a roommate."

He frowns. "What's that supposed to mean?"

"It means you were fine without me, and you were able to move on with Lanie like I knew you always would," I bite back. I don't know why I even said that. I guess I'm irritated she was there for him, and I wasn't.

"She was my roommate, May," he huffs.

"So, you're telling me that nothing has happened between you two since we were together?" I focus on his eyes, like I can see straight inside his head.

Releasing a frustrated sound, he puts his elbows on the counter, yanks at his hair and stares at me with a defeated expression.

"Alright, just one time," he says softly.

"Okay." It's fine. I'm fine. He hasn't been mine for a long time.

"That's it? Okay?" He mocks me by giving an I don't care shrug.

"What do you want me to do, Nico? Cry and scream at you? We weren't together."

He stands up out of the barstool like he's going to leave. "I'm going to tell you anyway. I waited an entire year for you to talk to me, and you never did. All I thought about was you. Lanie was around, and she didn't care about me like that anymore, but she let me use her. I didn't realize I was using her until afterward, and I was so fucking ashamed by what I did, but you were gone."

Why didn't I contact him like I wanted to? "If it makes you feel better I haven't dated or slept with anyone."

Groaning, he turns his head away from mine. "It doesn't. It only makes me feel worse."

Nico walks toward the door and leaves, slamming it behind him. I sit there and don't want this to be déjà vu and us never talking again. At a fast pace, I haul open the door, and he's standing outside gazing out at the parking lot.

Whirling around, Nico sees the look on my face and my eyes welling with tears. "Are you okay? I needed some air, that's all." Nico shouldn't be worrying about me, but he's still putting others' feelings ahead of his own.

I take a step toward him. "What I said that day, I didn't mean any of it. Please don't leave. Please don't not talk to me. I want your friendship back. I was… I was … so messed up after everything. The only reason I still talk to Jessie is because she kept pestering me the whole time the first year. Otherwise, I probably wouldn't have contacted her either."

Leaning against one of the pillars, Nico chews on the edge of his lower lip. "I should've called or texted, but I thought I was doing the right thing by letting you contact me when you were ready."

"Honestly, I didn't feel okay until after about a year, and then I thought it was too late." I pause. "Do you ever think about Ruby?" I run my hand against the side of my face and chin.

Nico's eyes meet mine with sympathy. "I do. I think about what would've happened if she didn't die—where we would be at now. The thing is, what happened, happened, and the past ended the way it did. I'm not mad at you. And it never would've been too late. Not for me, May."

I nod.

"I have to get ready for work, but can I talk to you later?"

I give him another nod.

"Okay, I'll talk to you then." I nod again. Am I some sort of puppet, and all I can do is nod?

Turning around, I walk back inside and close the door behind me. I slam my back against the door, and I slowly let myself melt to the floor until my legs are flat against the carpet. I pull my knees back to my chest and let out a small sob. I haven't felt like this in a while. It's like I'm back at age seventeen in a hole.

I'm not stuck in this hole with a cement covering on top, though. This time, it's loose grains of sand that I'm able to push myself through, and I do. Relief pours over me as I think about Nico's last few sentences—he isn't mad at me.

Lifting myself off the floor, I head into the bathroom and take a shower that's a little hotter than normal, but the burn feels good against my skin and dilutes my thoughts.

When I step out of the shower, I finish unpacking my room and organize the closet. Then I set up my art supplies, pull out my old sketchbooks, and dig until I find the one I'm looking for.

I open it up to the first time I sketched Nico. I could never get rid of this, not in a million years. This is the first time I've looked at it since we were dating. He appears younger here, not only because he was younger, but now he looks a little rougher around the edges with a hidden story.

These emotions make me feel like painting, and I have two blank canvases sitting in the corner of my room. Setting one up, I get all my paint ready and grab a brush to paint as I've never painted before.

I'm not sure how much time has passed, but my phone beeps. I wash my hands at the sink thoroughly, removing the paint, before picking up the phone and reading a text from Jessie.

Jessie: I've got big news!

Me: It can't be bigger than the engagement, right?

Jessie: Since it will be a while before we get married, Henry bought us plane tickets to go on a vacation this summer!

Me: Lucky! Where are you guys going?

Jessie: To see you, silly!

What? Is she serious?

Me: Are you serious? That doesn't sound like much of a vacation to me. But if you're serious, I'm so achingly happy!

Jessie: Yes! We'll be there in July!

I can't believe it. We text back and forth for a little longer, and then she calls me when she realizes I'm not at work. So we talk on the phone for about an hour.

Jessie had been telling Henry since she met him how she wanted to visit me. He finished his schooling last year and quickly found a job and had been saving up for a while.

Unlike Jessie, Henry's a big saver when it comes to money. He has been holding on to money from his previous jobs and has always had a big savings from what she says.

After I get off the phone with her, I put away all my old sketchbooks inside the box, finding a spot in the corner of the closet for it to go. The closet is the main thing I like about this apartment. It's huge. Back in my old room, you couldn't even walk in my closet because it was so small.

Strolling into the living room, I start the movie from where I drifted off, and it doesn't get any better, but I manage to truck my way through it. Then I type up the paper for class about it, but I kind of have to lie my way through it. I don't necessarily want to say this is the worst movie I have ever seen in my entire life. That's saying a lot because I've seen some terrible movies with Jessie.

When I finish the paper, I can't control my thoughts from drifting back to Nico, which my brain has been trying to avoid because I know friendship will never be enough. I'll want more than that.

# Chapter Twenty-One

*I*'ve been lying down in bed since eight. Yes, eight at night, and I'm only twenty years old—I realize I have no life.

A strum of a guitar awakens me, reaching out to my very soul, as I'm finally drifting off to sleep. These walls are paper thin, and it's more like a liquid barrier than an actual wall. I stretch to grab my phone off the side table to see what time it is. It's only nine. It feels like I've been lying here for more than an hour.

Besides the slight muffle of the guitar the wall traps, it sounds perfect. I pull the sheets away, step out of bed and walk toward the wall to sit with my back propped up against it, pressing my head back to get a better listen.

The barrier echoes a slight vibration that penetrates my bones all the way to the marrow. After about ten minutes, Nico stops playing.

I stand up and pick my phone up from the side table. After a quick debate with myself, I scroll through the names until I get to Nico. I added his name back after I saw him the first day here.

Me: Play a song for me?

I think maybe he didn't hear the text, or maybe he chose to ignore it, but then a soft melody drifts through the wall. He plays the same lovely song he first played for me way back at my house. I feel now the same way I did then—the same way I have always felt. I never once told him those three simple, yet not easy, words. They spoke in my head endless times but never aloud.

When he's finished playing, he sends me a text, and the beep yanks me from my trance.

Nico: Any more requests this evening?

I don't even change out of my pajamas. Slipping on a pair of flats, I leave my apartment. When I reach his door, I knock, and he answers in a pair of jeans and a black T-shirt with his hair rumpled.

"I prefer to listen without the wall—if that's okay?" *Please don't slam the door in my face.* But I don't believe he will.

Nico gives me a small smile. "It's more than okay." He holds the door open for me, and I step over the threshold into his apartment.

I look around his living room, and it's nice. Inside, there are two brown recliners and a green couch. Not the modern recliners that are stiff, but the super comfortable ones that are big and feel like you're melting into a perfectly shaped cloud.

Needing to sit in one immediately, I dive right into it, and the chair is like heaven, molding to my body perfectly. Kicking the chair back, I breathe deeply. "Sorry, Nico. I had to. You don't understand. All I have is a futon!"

Chuckling, he saunters over and sits in the other one. "You can take one with you if you want."

A big grin crosses my face. "I might have to take you up on that offer. I'm not just saying that either, I will most likely confiscate this chair for myself."

His TV is huge, and he has a large case filled with hundreds of movies. "I might have to take most of those, too." I point.

"Nope. I have my limit with that one."

Closing the footrest of the chair, I twist it side to side. Okay, not only is it the most comfortable recliner I have ever sat in, but it spins. You can't get much better than that.

"Did you just get home from work?" I stop spinning.

"No. After I got off work, I went to my parents' for dinner since Mom made stew. There's leftovers in the fridge if you want some." He nods in the direction of the fridge.

"I'm going to take you up on that offer." Charlotte's cooking is amazing, and her food brings all my taste buds to life.

"I spent most of the day training John."

My eyes widen. "Are we talking about John-John?"

He laughs. "Yes, you were way off about him. He's still there, and he's training for the manager position."

I shake my head. "I can't believe this. I feel so bad." I shouldn't have been so judgmental about him, but I seriously thought he wouldn't last past a week, and then I thought for sure he would be gone before a year. It's nice to be proven wrong about people.

"Nah, don't worry. I was with you in that same boat."

I push up from the chair, not sure which direction to go. "Where do we go so I can listen to the rest of the jam session?"

He shakes his head. "This way." I follow him to the

bedroom on the right. "There's not much going on in here right now because I only moved a few things in here after Lanie left."

I don't even get jealous when he mentions Lanie. Okay, I'm lying, maybe a smidge jealous.

A guitar rests on a chair, and I sit down on the floor in front of it. He offers me the chair, but I let him have it so he can sit and play. He strums a couple of slow and beautiful songs for me, and then we sit and talk for a long while about nothing, but it's everything.

I pull out my phone to look at the time, and it's already close to eleven. "I better go. Otherwise, I won't be able to wake up in the morning. Anytime I stay up past ten and have to wake up early, I'm tired no matter what."

He stands up out of the chair to lead me from the bedroom and then turns back around. "Oh, I forgot to ask you… Violet is having this show tomorrow, if you want to go."

"Isn't Violet in New York?" I ask.

"Yeah, but she wanted to do a hometown show with a lot of her artwork. It's going to be at the museum tomorrow night."

I'm proud and amazed by this. "Like her own private show there?"

He rolls his eyes. "You should see how excited she is about it. It's more cockiness really."

"I'll go. What time is it?"

He chews on the side of his lip and thinks about it. "I think it's at seven. I'll double check with her on that. You can ride with me, so you don't have to waste gas driving out there."

I shrug, fighting a smile. "That works. Now that that's

settled, onto more important matters. I'm going to have to take that stew."

Strolling toward the fridge, Nico pulls out the container and hands me his precious stew—which I gladly accept. He walks me out even with my apartment being right next door, and we stand there for a while with our gazes locked. I finally say, "Well, I'll see you tomorrow."

Should I hug him or something? I want to, but maybe it's way too soon for hugs for him.

"See you tomorrow, May."

I tell him bye and head inside. The first thing I do is stick the food in the fridge, right in front on the top shelf so I won't forget it for work tomorrow.

Hopping back into bed, ignoring the butterflies in my stomach, I get all nestled in when my phone beeps.

Nico: Goodnight

Me: Goodnight

♥

When my alarm goes off, I feel like the dead have risen. I get ready and grab the stew which I almost forgot, but thank goodness at the last second I remember. The memories from the night before come rushing back, and I smile to myself.

After I arrive at work, the first thing I do is stop by Mom's office to catch up. "Guess what?"

Lifting her head, Mom stops typing. "Hey, sweetheart. What's going on?"

"Jessie is coming to town sometime next month!" I squeal.

Mom squeals along with me. "Aw, I'm going to see my second daughter. One of her first stops will be the house. Got it?"

I lean against the doorframe. "We're also going to meet Henry in person, finally."

Mom taps her index finger on her desk like she's pounding a dent in it. "You better believe I'm going to have all sorts of questions for him."

"I'll let her know." I leave Mom's office and head to mine.


Me: Mom is going to grill Henry when you guys come into town.

Jessie: Lol! I'll have him prepped for that.


At lunch when I'm eating in the breakroom with Mom, she asks, "What do you think about me going on a date with someone?"

I stop chewing my stew. "What are we talking about? Did someone ask you on a date, or did you ask someone on a date?"

Mom looks like she doesn't want to have this conversation with me, but I'm fine if she wants to date someone else. It has been over three years.

"Eric asked me out on a date."

My eyebrows shoot to my hairline. "Do I know this Eric? I don't even know an Eric."

She takes a sip of her drink and sets it back down. "You know Eric, he lives down the street toward the end."

I think hard about it, scanning the street in my mind. "Nope. I have no idea who this Eric is."

She sighs. "Black truck—his wife Abbie passed away a

little over a year ago."

Wouldn't I have remembered someone dying? Maybe she didn't tell me this, or maybe because I have no idea who these people are, it must have gone in one ear and out the other. Mom knows the whole neighborhood. I only know Mrs. Jenkins.

"There are a lot of people with black vehicles, including me."

"I'm going to ignore that remark. So, what do you think?" She stares at me, waiting for me to give her an answer.

I think maybe she should do it if she wants to. "I say, do whatever you want to do. If you want to be independent, I'll back you up. If you want to try going out with this guy, I won't act like a bratty child. If he's a jerk, that will be a whole different story."

Mom purses her lips, silently debating. "I'm going to have to think about it."

When she says that, we both know she's going to end up saying yes.

The rest of work flies by, and all I can think about is tonight. I'm not only excited about going with Nico, but I can't wait to see Violet.

It's been a year since I last saw her, and it feels too long.


Me: What should I wear tonight?

Jessie: I can't believe I don't get to go to this show. Can't you tell Violet to have it next month? Better yet, tell her to have another show when I come into town.

Me: I'll let her know, but no promises. You know Violet.

Jessie: I'd say wear a dress, a really short dress.

Me: I'm going to pass on that, but I will do a skirt.

Searching through my closet, I sort through what I have. Most of my dresses and skirts look like clothes for work, which they are.

I pull out the black and white, pinstripe, pencil skirt that comes right above my knees, and a black short sleeve blouse. I pair that with my black and white Converse, so I don't look like I'm going to a business interview. Finishing off my look, I add eyeshadow, mascara, and a clear lip gloss. Observing myself in the mirror, I decide to leave my hair down.

My phone makes a beeping sound, and I check it.

Nico: The show does start at seven. I'll come by at six-thirty. Does that work for you?

Me: Yes, that sounds good.

A knock comes at my door around six-twenty. As I open the door, I find Nico dressed in jeans and a T-shirt. I probably should've worn jeans instead.

"Should I change into something else?" I ask as I pull at the bottom of my shirt.

He scans me up and down. "No, you look perfect. I'm probably going to be the one up there standing out, but I don't have time to go fancy myself up."

I let out a laugh. I don't know, he looks pretty good in his jeans and shirt. I grab my bag before we leave, and he walks me to his truck to open the door for me. He hasn't lost his gentleman ways.

# Chapter Twenty-Two

When we arrive at the museum, we park several streets away, but I don't mind the walk. "Are your parents coming?" I ask.

"Yeah, they should already be here," Nico says as he opens his truck door.

The wind is taking my hair and blowing it every which way—I should've pulled it back. A reminder note will be—to keep hair ties in my purse for future occasions.

"Do they mind I'm coming?" I haven't seen them since Ruby's funeral, and I'm not sure what they think about me anymore. Nico's parents were always laid back and welcoming whenever I saw them. They never asked too many questions and always offered me food and more food when I'd go over there. The circumstance for the food was understandable with me being pregnant at the time.

"No, Mom is glad to see you again. She's asked about you a lot."

I hit a crack and stumble—Nico catches my arm. "Okay, they need to fix this," I mumble. "This sidewalk is a disaster waiting to happen." Small hairline cracks and full-on craters fill the entire sidewalk. "Sorry about that. I'm nervous about seeing your parents. It's been a long time."

"Don't worry so much." Nico doesn't loosen his grip on my arm for several seconds.

I can't help it. I'm laid back about a lot of things, but this is different. This is Nico's parents we're talking about.

As we reach the door to the art museum, the glass is covered in greasy handprints everywhere. I can understand the lower section because kids don't understand, but there are handprints way above the door handle. I kind of want to buy glass cleaner and spritz it down.

I haven't been to the art museum in forever. The last time was before ninth grade—with Dad. Mom stayed home, so it was only the two of us.

We were there for hours and hours, and we still didn't see everything. If we'd wanted to go faster through the exhibits, we could've, but Dad liked to take it all in. He had a way of making each piece a distorted maze and figuring it out on his own by trying out a different turn.

I'm not that intense when it comes to art. I look at a painting, and I either like it or I don't. I prefer to think more about the person behind the art, like what they look like, or what they were thinking at the time they did the artwork versus figuring out what it means.

The museum desk is to the right, and a young guy with glasses sits behind it. His hair is gelled to the side with a little too much plastered throughout. "Can I help you?" he asks as we approach.

Nico places his hands on the desk and smiles. "We're here

for Violet Evitts' show. I'm her brother."

The guy's head dips forward and his gaze lowers to look down at Nico, even though Nico is standing above him, and this guy is sitting down. I glance at the guy's name tag. In big uppercase font, the name Gavin is displayed. Gavin seems to be a douche.

"And?" No, not seems to be, *is*.

Nico looks at me like 'who is this guy?' "Well, Gavin, I'm supposed to be meeting Violet for her show."

Gavin tilts his head to the side. "Do you have your tickets?"

Nico taps his fingers at a quick pace on the desk. "What tickets? Violet told me to come up here and tell you I'm her brother, and that's it."

"Um. There have been several people already who have come in here saying they're Violet's relatives."

This guy is getting on my nerves. "Does she have a list with the name Nico on it?" I ask.

Darting his eyes between both of us, Gavin then studies the list sitting right in front of him. Bringing his pinky toward the list, he slowly glides it down the paper until it comes to an abrupt stop on Nico's name.

"Last name?"

"Evitts. Like Violet's last name." Nico is frustrated and tries to say it politely.

"Why didn't you say you had a list?" I point at the sheet of paper on the desk in front of us.

Gavin stares at me like I'm the idiot. "Only those who are on the list know that a list exists."

I highly doubt that's true. A lot of places have lists with

guests on it. I nod, as if he has all the perfect answers.

Gavin looks at me with a bored expression. "And you are?"

"She's my plus one. Isn't that obvious?" Nico slides his hand off the desk.

Gavin purses his lips. "No, not really. Your plus one could've already arrived or might arrive later."

"Is my plus one marked off?"

Gavin studies the list. "No."

Shaking his head, Nico has had enough. "She's my plus one. Now, can you tell me where we go?"

Gavin hands us two stickers with our names written on it. He writes, Nico's plus one on mine. Not sure why he couldn't ask me my name and write that, but whatever. He then points us toward the stairs and tells us to take the first left and then the second right.

Peeling my sticker off, I slap it on my chest and walk toward the trash can a few feet away to toss the paper part in. Nico follows me. "What an idiot."

"I guess he's trying to do things the correct way, but he still didn't have to be ridiculous about the entire process," I say.

I peer down at my sticker on my blouse one more time and shake my head. New people trail in, and they don't seem to be at the desk with Gavin as long as we were. They do have tickets in their hands, though.

We ascend the stairs, and I gaze at the artwork on the walls along the way. They have changed this place a lot since I was here last. I might have to schedule a full day one weekend to view the local artists' artwork lining these long, tall walls.

After following Gavin's directions, we arrive in front of huge double doors at the end of the hall that are open wide. Conversations spill out the doors and echo in the hallway.

There are so many people here to see Violet's work. "Wow, there's a full crowd tonight."

"Yeah, my parents told everyone they know and told them to tell people that they know. Violet also keeps in touch with everyone through social media and has a shit ton of followers."

That makes sense. I'm going to have to look up Violet's profiles and see what all she has on there. I bet her status updates are hilarious, even though she's not trying to be.

Scanning the room, I laser in on a purple head across the room, and Violet's hair isn't short anymore. It's more of a bob, which is still considered short but long for her. In all the old pictures I saw around Nico and Violet's house she always had short hair. "She still has the purple hair, I see."

"I think she's going to color her hair purple until the day she dies."

"I think she is, too." I can't imagine her with any other hair color.

I survey the room, and maybe I'm underdressed. Some of these women have on the tallest heels I've ever seen in my life. If I wore those, I'd look like an Amazonian giant compared to everyone else here.

"Come on. Let's talk to Violet and let her know we're here." Nico tugs on my elbow, then releases it—I wish he would've continued to hold onto it.

Violet's wearing purple slacks with a matching purple blazer that has black ruffles at the end of her sleeves. It looks great on her.

"Hey, Violet," I say when we approach her.

She whips around like a tornado. "I know that voice."

Violet scans me over and then Nico, her eyes lingering on him with a glare. "What's going on? Nico, you didn't tell me you were bringing May. Have we gone back in a time machine?"

Nico waves his hands in the air. "Surprise!"

I smack Nico's arm. "I thought you told them I was coming."

"No. I told you I told my parents you were coming." He grins.

Now, Violet smacks Nico's arm. "What the hell, man?"

"You didn't tell me about your secret meeting last year." Nico shrugs.

Violet stares hard at him and then smacks my arm softly. "You told me not to say anything, and then you tell him?"

"It sort of slipped out in class." I cringe. I would've told Nico eventually, but I didn't mean for it to come out accidentally.

Violet twirls her hand in the air. "Over it. New subject. What's going on here?" She points between the two of us.

"She's my neighbor." Nico beams.

"Whatever. I need real answers here." Violet's hands land on her hips.

I can't help but grin. "I like your outfit. This is the best you've ever looked."

Slowly, she runs her hand through her hair. "I know. There's this girl I've been hanging out with in New York, and she made this for me." She rubs her palm up and down the sleeve of her blazer.

I search around the room like I know exactly who she's talking about. "Is she here, too?"

"No, she had some stuff she needed to finish up for a couple of clients before the weekend."

"Nico? Is that May?" I hear a voice from behind me and quickly turn around at the same time Nico does.

Nico's parents are standing right there. Charlotte and Tim. What do I do? What do I say? Before I can say anything, Charlotte pulls me in for a big squeeze and whispers in my ear, "I've missed you."

Please don't let me cry in front of all these people. I tell her I missed her, too, which I have. When she pulls back, I give Tim a wave. *Please don't pull me into a hug. It will be too weird.* He does offer me an awkward handshake, but it feels nice.

Charlotte turns to Violet and squeezes the life out of her. I think her mom may pop her like a purple grape. "I'm so proud of my baby."

Shaking her head, Violet politely skates away from the hug. "Mom, I haven't been a baby, since, well, since I was a baby."

"Don't give me that." Charlotte rubs Violet's back, as if she's going to sit her in her lap and start trying to burp her.

I'm sure Mom would be acting the same way if I had moved off to New York and came back to visit. She's already acting that way now, and I'm still in the same city and see her every day.

"I'm going to warn you guys that this show is past and present, so you two celebrities are proudly displayed on the wall over there." Violet points between Nico and me and then at the wall to our left.

I look to where she's pointing, and there the drawing of me and Nico is on full display. "Shut up." I turn to her. "You still have that?"

"Of course." She shrugs. "I can't let go of a masterpiece."

Nico is already walking over to look at the picture. "You didn't tell me she was going to have that," I say as I hurry next to him.

He glances at me and shakes his head. "You know Violet. She's top secret with a lot of things." Violet may not talk a lot about herself, but everything about her shows throughout her artwork.

Nico slides his hands into his pockets. "Do you remember that day?"

"Perfectly." I remember every detail about it. The way I didn't know Nico but felt comfortable with him then—the same as I do now.

We stand in silence, gazing at the drawing for a long time. Something started between us that day. It may have even begun when I went for my job interview, and his head first popped up from behind the counter. And it's beginning to form a shape of its own once again.

You can blow into a balloon and watch it inflate, and then release it and see it deflate. You can take that same balloon and blow into it again and observe it inflating. That's what my heart is doing in this moment, inflating and holding the air.

Nico's pinky finger brushes my hand, and I brush his right back with mine.

# Chapter Twenty-Three

The night before when I saw Nico's family, it had me missing old times even more, but it felt great. I felt better than I have in a long time.

After work, I went home, got ready for class and drove to the college campus.

When I walk into the classroom, Nico is already there. He's reading a book and listening to music again. My heart picks up the pace just from the sight of him.

I sit down next to him as he pulls out his earbuds and spreads them across his desk. "You ready for the quiz?" he asks.

Fishing a pen out of my backpack, I set it on the desk in front of me. "If I can remember it all. I finished watching the movie and don't remember exactly everything I watched."

Nico taps the eraser of his pencil against the desk. "I don't think the next movie is going to get much better. I didn't make it all the way through the first one."

We chit chat back and forth before Mr. Hendricks strolls into the classroom. Instantly, he passes out the quiz—no duck tie today, but it does have chickens on it. I shake my head to myself and laugh. Nico meets my gaze and mouths, "What?"

Nodding in Mr. Hendricks' direction, I point at my chest, and Nico still has no idea what I'm talking about. "I'll tell you later."

Sliding the quiz closer to me, I scan down the page and quickly read all ten questions. Easy peasy—I got this. I take my quiz, walk to the front, and hand it to the professor. Then I unzip my backpack to pull out my essay to turn in at the separate stack of papers.

Mr. Hendricks gives a smile. "See you next week."

That's it? I knew we were going to take a quiz, but I thought he was going to teach or talk about it. Fine by me.

I go out in the hall and press my back against the wall while waiting for Nico. About ten minutes later, he walks out. "Finally!"

"You didn't have to wait for me." He smiles.

With a shrug, I start walking off, and Nico pulls the handle of my backpack, drawing me back to him. My chest flutters happily, and I laugh.

"So, what were you laughing about in there?"

Turning around to face him, I point at my chest. "Did you see the tie?"

"You mean the chickens?" Nico glances toward the doorway.

"Yes!" I practically jump in the air.

"I think I need to get one of those for myself."

"You should." He would look cute in a chicken tie.

"I didn't realize we would get out so early. Do you want to come over and start on the other movie?" I ask as we walk down the hall.

"Not really," he says, and I frown back at him. "I mean, I

don't want to watch the next movie, but I'll come over and watch it with you." I like that answer.

"Okay." I search the parking lot and find his truck parked in a front space. "I see you were able to score VIP parking again."

"Let me guess. You're parked way out there again?" He points at the back of the parking lot.

"You guessed correctly. What do I owe you?" I pretend to pull out a wallet.

He tilts his head to the side thinking hard about my question. "A pizza?"

"You want me to buy us a pizza on the way back?" I'm hungry, no, I'm starving.

"No, I will. After you get in my truck and let me drive you to your car."

"Again, I'm going to pass on that, but I'll see you back at my place. By the way, I like supreme minus the mushrooms." I start backing away from Nico.

"That technically isn't a supreme, then."

Pulling my arms up, I cross them in front of my chest. "Okay, smarty pants, what's it called?"

Nico chews on the side of his lip. "Uh, one less topping supreme?"

"Whatever, you're a nerd. See you in a little bit." I wave and walk to my car, shaking my head to myself. Talking with him is so easy.

Tossing my backpack in the passenger seat, I start the engine and lower my head to the steering wheel. What am I doing? I haven't felt this good about something in a long time.

I make it to my place before Nico arrives, and I pull out

the list of movies we're watching in class. Finding the one for week two, I locate it on my phone and press rent it now. Maybe this one won't be so bad, since it isn't an old war movie. Again, it isn't a movie I've heard of, though. *Where is this guy finding these movies?*

Mom isn't as old as Mr. Hendricks, but I read her the list of movies we're supposed to watch in class. Her response was, "Did you just make those names up?"

Right after I order the movie and set it up on the TV, Nico knocks on the door. I let him in, and he's carrying the pizza in one hand, a big bottle of soda and a white paper bag in the other.

I take the pizza from him and set it on the counter.

As I'm reaching in the cupboard for two glasses, he hands me the white paper bag. "What's this?" I ask.

Nico sits down on one of the barstools. "I forgot to give it to you in class. I picked it up when I was on break today."

Excitement and anxiousness set in, and I unfold the bag to look inside. "You didn't!"

"I did."

The bag is filled with all things white chocolate from Pete's Candy and More. Yanking out a square of white chocolate filled with peanut butter, I groan loudly as I take the hugest bite in my life.

Nico flicks his eyes back and forth from me to the candy, so I thrust the bag at him. "Eat one. And thank you."

He sets the candy on top of the counter. "Don't worry, I got a bag of brown chocolate all to myself. That baby is all yours." I'm secretly thrilled he doesn't eat any—I'm a little greedy when it comes to white chocolate.

Nico opens the lid to the pizza. "Here's your one less topping supreme pizza."

I kick his foot with mine and start pouring the soda. "Did Violet already leave?"

He pulls out a piece of pizza. "Yeah, she left this afternoon but first stopped by the bookstore to make sure I was handling things correctly. She said I was doing a pretty good job at running the place, but not as good of a job as her."

Laughing, I shake my head. Before we left the show last night, Violet told me I had better start texting her, and she should only have to tell me that one time. I plan on texting her this weekend after she's back in town and already settled.

While we're eating, my phone dings. I set down my slice of pizza and pick up the phone. "Sorry. Let me text Jessie back, or she'll keep texting."

"Tell her I said hey."

I set the phone down on the countertop before I read her entire message. "Did I tell you she's getting married?"

"No? To who?" Nico puts his pizza on his plate.

"His name is Henry, and he seems good for her. They're coming down in July if you want to meet up."

"Sounds good to me." He goes back to eating.

Picking up my phone again, I press the home button.


Jessie: I know it's far away, but I picked the colors for the bridesmaid's dresses. I'm going with blue. You can pick out what shade of blue and what style.

Me: Great! Nico told me to tell you hey.

Jessie: What????????????? He's there now?

Jessie: Am I interrupting something?

Jessie: I am, aren't I?

Me: Um, we're sitting here eating pizza and about to watch a movie for class.

Jessie: Sure, you are.  Just a reminder, protection is key.

Me: Talk to you tomorrow.

She's crazy. I place my phone on the counter next to Nico's cellphone and finish eating my pizza. "Sorry about that."

"I don't mind."

Nico finishes his fourth slice of pizza, and I finish my second. Then I grasp the bag of candy and dive into it. The last time I went to Pete's was right after the ultrasound when we found out the baby was going to be a girl.

*Nico dropped Mom off after the appointment, and we still had about an hour and a half until we had to be at work.*

*Nico took my hand from my lap. "What are you thinking about? The baby?"*

*I felt guilty when he asked that question. Was I supposed to be thinking about the baby? We had recently found out it was a girl. I was fine with it being a boy or a girl. I only wanted the baby to be healthy, which everything looked good from the ultrasound.*

*"No, Nico, I was thinking about the white chocolate candy from Pete's." I pulled my hand back from his and brought them both to my face. "I'm going to be the worst mom on the planet. I'm still a teenager and am over here selfishly thinking*

*about candy."*

*He laughed so hard that I grew frustrated and wanted to throw him out of the car. "Did you think that maybe it's Ruby thinking about the candy and not you?"*

*I folded my hands in my lap. "You're only trying to make me feel better for being a selfish, delusional teenager that has no idea what she's doing."*

*He grew serious. "None of us know what we're doing. My mom admitted to me that she still doesn't know what she's doing half the time now. We're in a shitty boat and just have to make it to landfall."*

*"What if that boat sinks?" I groaned.*

*"Then I'll toss you a life jacket, and we'll have to swim to shore."*

*I brought my hand back down to his. "Thanks for making me feel better. I'm not sure how long it will last, but I still want to eat that chocolate."*

*"Don't you fret, and don't you fret either, Ruby." He moved his index finger up and down at my stomach, as if the baby could see it.*

Nico may have been young—he still is—but he would've been a great dad. However, I would've been screwing up all over the place, but he wouldn't have been.

I eat half the bag of candy and then roll it up, putting it away. Otherwise, I'll eat the whole thing and I want to save some for tomorrow.

We sit on the couch, and I start the movie. The beginning score screams the nineteen-seventies.

My phone beeps, and I don't get up to answer it. Then it beeps again. "I'm going to turn it off."

"You don't have to do that," Nico says.

"Otherwise, Jessie will keep interrupting this glorious movie that my brain particles need to focus on." I get up and snatch the phone off the counter.

Before I realize which phone I picked up, I click the home screen. I stare at it for a little too long until the phone fades to black, and then I click it again. It's the picture Violet took of Nico and me before she started sketching us that day. Turning my head, I look at Nico who is still facing the TV.

Do I say anything? Do I say nothing? I don't want him to think I'm going through his phone, but I'm not going to pretend I didn't see this. Walking to the futon, I hold out the photo in front of his face when I reach him. "What's this?"

"What's what?" He turns to the phone, and his eyebrows raise. He leaps off the couch, and I pull away from him before he can confiscate the phone. "Shit."

Giggling, I dart toward my room, and he yanks me back by my waist. I make a move to tear away from his grip, and he tugs me backward. Somehow, we both end up tripping, and he hits the floor with me safely landing on him like he's my own pillow of safety.

I lie there breathing hard, his chest against my back breathing just as fast, and then he rips the phone from my hand.

# Chapter Twenty-Four

My hand feels the emptiness from Nico tearing the phone away. "Hey!" I yell and roll off him.

Pulling up on my side, I watch as he rubs the back of his neck while slightly frowning. "Sorry about that."

"Why do you have that on your background?" I'm secretly thrilled that he does. My heart is pounding at a rapid pace that has me desperate for an answer.

"Violet," he groans and releases a sigh while looking up at the ceiling in frustration.

Standing, I brush the invisible dust from my pants. "Oh." I was hoping it would've been because he still feels something for me.

While staring at me, Nico fiddles around with his phone, passing it back and forth between both his hands. "I don't want you to get creeped out or think I'm weird or anything."

"Why would I? I still have the drawing of you that I drew in my closet." I leave out the part about me sitting there gazing at it with longing. Maybe I should leave the art world and become a poet or a terrible comedian.

"You do?" A smile forms on his face, and it tilts up on one side.

"Don't change the subject, but yes." I flick him softly on his chest.

Nico lets out a long breath before speaking. "Okay, after the day you left when Violet drew the picture, I snatched her phone and texted myself the photo of us. Ridiculous, right? I barely knew you at the time, but I knew I wanted to save that picture."

"I've heard worse." I laugh and take a seat on the barstool.

Nico pulls out the other stool and sits beside me. "Still. So I kept this photo on my camera roll, even when I got a new phone. I don't look at it all the time, but there were times when I'd think about you, and I wanted to see your face. There are plenty of photos I have of us, but this is the one that means the most to me."

That day meant a lot to me, too. I think about actions and how so many things happened that shouldn't have. Would I have met Nico if my dad hadn't shot himself? I want to say in some way, I still would've met him. Eventually, I would've gone by Jessie's work to see her and might've bumped into him there.

"And you set it as your background?" I prop my elbow on the countertop and plop my head against my hand, hiding my smile.

"No! That was Violet. She did it sometime today before she left. I thought she was over the whole going through my phone phase, but I guess not. I haven't had time to take the picture off. That's all." He looks nervous. Why does he look nervous?

"That's all?" I grin.

"Yes."

"Okay." I shrug.

"Okay?"

"That's what I just said."

He shakes his head and stands up from the barstool. "You're still annoying, you know that?"

Hopping off the seat, I bump his shoulder with mine. "Annoying, huh?"

"And cute." Nico reaches up toward me, brushing the hair back from my face that has fallen forward.

"Animals are cute." My shoulders droop.

"You know you're beautiful, alright?" He smiles.

The smile slips from my face, and suddenly I feel sad. Nico has been everything I've ever wanted, even when I was lost in every single emotional state known to mankind. I should've opened the door and run after him in my driveway and told him I just needed a little time to myself.

"What?" he says softly, moving closer to me, the smile leaving his face.

"I'm sorry, Nico. I'm sorry for that day. I'm sorry I didn't try talking to you sooner. I'm sorry that everything was my fault." The waterworks start, and I can't shut them off.

Wrapping his arms around me, he holds me tight. "I thought about texting you so many damn times, and I should've. You didn't do anything wrong—you know that, right? And Ruby was nobody's fault, you hear me?"

I nod against his shoulder. "I know that now, but I didn't know that then. I couldn't get there on my own, and it took so long. There's only ever been you, Nico."

Releasing me, he takes a step back, running his hands through his hair before turning away from me. "And that's where you're better than me. I should've waited for you instead of sleeping with Lanie. Everything about that was wrong."

I step toward him and wrap my arms around his waist, pressing my chest against his back. I wouldn't have cared if he had dated a thousand girls while we weren't together because that's the thing, we weren't together anymore. Okay, that's a lie, a thousand would be a bit extreme. The point is he's here now, and I'm here.

"Nico, no one would've waited around three years after the way I treated you. In fact, I'm surprised you're even talking to me now."

"That's because I love you, May." He doesn't turn around and look at me when he says it. I absorb the beautiful words like a sponge and will hold them in for the rest of my life.

I lift my cheek from the comfort of the back of his shoulder and pull my arms out from around his waist. Walking around to look at him face to face, I slide my hands against his cheeks. "I have loved you since I don't even know when, but I did, and I do. That was my biggest regret this whole time—not letting you know that."

"I was going to tell you on prom night, but I didn't want to ruin anything." Nico brushes his hand against mine.

"No, I should've told you then, too. I wanted to," I say.

I don't have time to react—Nico's lips crash against mine, and he backs me up all the way until I hit the back of the door. His lips mold perfectly to mine, and our kisses are like they were three years ago, if not better.

Our mouths open simultaneously, and Nico's tongue meets mine. A hand slides under the back of my shirt—it's warm against my skin, and I feel consumed by it. His other hand is around my neck, my hair intertwined with his fingers. I love the way his words, touch, and kiss all make me feel.

Running my hands along the edge of his shirt, I grip the bottom and start to haul it up his back. In one swift motion, Nico lifts me in his arms, carrying me to the futon, and I let out a small squeal. Does this really happen with people getting carried? I guess it does tonight.

Before he can lie me down on the futon, I yelp. "No, not the futon! It's too uncomfortable. The bedroom." I laugh while pointing at my door.

"Ugh. I don't know if I can carry you to the bedroom. I barely made it here." He chuckles with his voice straining.

"Maybe if I was five feet that would help out a little." I drop down from his arms, and his body relaxes. I grab onto the front of his shirt at his chest and drag him to my room where zero action has ever taken place, but it's going to now.

He yanks me down to the bed with him, and I roll him over to sit on top of him. This time I succeed at tugging his shirt up his back and over his head.

Nico draws my waist against his hips, and he rocks me back and forth against him. I kiss him with every part of me there is, and I kiss him with so much strength and force making up for the time we've missed.

Pulling my shirt over my head, I toss it to the floor, and Nico runs his mouth across my jaw and down my neck. He reaches to the back of my bra where the clasp isn't there. Then he trails his fingers to the front, and he isn't able to get the clasp open. His head hits my chest, and he starts laughing. "God, I'm an idiot."

Lifting his head, I look him in the eye and smile before I kiss his mouth and undo the clasp at the same time while shimmying out of it.

The rest of our clothes get lost along the way. He attempts to roll me onto my back, but I don't let him. I want to prove to him how much I missed him, and I do.

♥

My alarm goes off from the living room where I left my phone. I don't want to get out of bed, but I have to. I scramble for my shirt and pants on the floor, but I'm not sure where my bra and underwear are—and I don't care. Nico is still dead to the world, even with my loud cellphone alarm going off in the other room.

In the living room, I slam my toe into one of the barstools when I reach for the phone in the dark. I stop the alarm and see the two missed texts from Jessie.

Rubbing my toe, I smile silently to myself thinking about what ruckus her texts caused.

Jessie: I forgot to tell you to tell Nico I said hello.

Jessie: If I'm interrupting anything, sorry. *wink wink*

She's insane. I laugh to myself.

Me: Thanks for the text last night.

I think about Nico and the night before, and I want to wake him up and do it all over again. I'm on birth control, and he had a condom, and we made sure we did everything safely.

One day I may be able to go through the whole pregnancy thing again, but it won't be for a very long time.

Jessie's probably still asleep and will most likely be texting me when I get to work. Speaking of work, I've got to get ready.

I walk into the kitchen and turn on the light, peering inside the bedroom. Nico is still asleep. I'll let him rest while I take a shower and then wake him or attempt to. So I shower and get dressed for work.

Exiting the bathroom, I bounce on the bed, and Nico makes a soft grunting noise while continuing to sleep. Well, this is fun.

"Nico?" I say loudly and move his arm back and forth. "Wake up!"

Opening his eyes, he rolls over to face me, then closes his eyes again. "I've got work. Do you want to stay here?"

Nico opens his eyes and pulls me down beside him, giving me a sweet kiss on the lips. "I wish I didn't have to leave this bed today, but I have to work later, too."

Sitting up, he rubs at his eye with the edge of his palm. I find his clothes on the floor and hand them to him.

After he finishes getting dressed, I walk him to the front door. "I'll see you tonight?" he asks.

"Of course, we have a movie to watch." I do a fist pump in the air over the false excitement of the movie for class.

Leaning forward, he gives me a soft kiss before leaving. I close the door and start to move away. Then there's a soft knock, and I turn back to pull open the door. Nico steps toward me with a fierce look in his eyes. Cradling my face in his hands, he kisses me with such intensity that my body is an endless wildfire that refuses to be extinguished. I kiss him back with the same magnitude, to the point where I may have to miss work.

He pulls back to examine my face. "Don't give up on me again, okay?"

"I won't." And I mean it. Then he's kissing me again.

# Chapter Twenty-Five

Yesterday, Nico and I went for the first time together to visit Ruby's grave. I may not have known how she would've turned out in life, but I can imagine. We stopped by Dad's, and I swapped out the flowers and stuck a couple of paint brushes in there in case he needs them where he is.

We brought our lunch there, and I did a few headstone rubbings at a couple of new graves. Nico brought his guitar and played a song for anyone out there who was listening.

Nico and I have been spending practically every day together—since we do happen to live next door to each other. We've both changed in ways that make the relationship better than it ever was.

I'm at the airport waiting for Jessie to arrive with Henry. The place is packed, and I had a brief meltdown not knowing how to get here. I parked in some money saving lot and had to take a bus from there.

Then I got inside and had no idea where to go. I asked around a lot, but I'm here now and holding up a sign for Jessie. This was her request, not mine. She wants to feel like a celebrity when she arrives with someone holding her name on a big poster board.

So, here I am—the only one holding up a sign, while people from the plane make their way out to meet whoever they came here to meet.

I'm watching people walk by—some are not meeting anyone, and others are hugging people. I don't see her, but then I hear her screeching through the entire airport. I turn my head in the direction of the scream, and she flies toward me with her blonde hair flapping everywhere.

Her arms wrap around me, squeezing me tight. "I can't believe I'm back!" She releases me and turns to find Henry. He's several feet back, walking our way. He didn't take the opportunity to run at me and screech—that would've been interesting.

"Henry, come on, we're missing precious time." Jessie waves him over.

He gives me a warm smile. "I'm glad to meet you finally. I hear about you all the time. With all the texting Jessie does with you, I feel like we already know each other."

Henry is tall with dark, smooth skin, and the best-looking cheekbones I have ever seen. I'm a little jealous about that. "I know. I see your pictures all the time, so it seems like I'm meeting someone I already know. It's kind of weird." I laugh.

We talk for a few minutes, and then I remember Violet. "Oh, I have a surprise for you, Jessie." I take out my phone and call her.

"This better be good." She claps her hands together, and I turn the phone around to face her as soon as Violet pops up on the screen.

I shimmy around so we can both see her. Violet is sitting there waiting for one of us to say something first.

"Violet!" Jessie screams.

Violet covers her ears and gives us a grin. "You think I'd be used to all the fan's reactions by now." Her hair is still cut in a bob, except with light purple color covered in darker purple streaks this time. "You look good, Jessie." Jessie keeps waving with excitement.

"Hey, Violet, we're right on time," I say.

"I already talk to you all the time, May. Where's this fiancé?" I swivel the phone and show her Henry's face.

"Hello." His voice is deep, and he smiles widely.

"Not a big talker, but you're quite the looker. I'm impressed. You know, I remember Jessie's taste in boys, and I'm glad to see this part of her life has greatly improved." Henry shoots Jessie and me a look like, *What is this girl talking about?*

I flip the phone from Henry back to us. "It's us again."

"I have to go." Violet points at the clock behind her. "I'm on a time crunch. Let's do this again sometime."

We tell each other bye and then hang up the phone.

"Do you guys want to rest for a while or what?" I fold up the sign and stuff it back in my bag.

Henry takes out his phone and checks the time. "We still need to pick up the car and check in at the hotel. Then after that, it's up to you two." He grasps Jessie's hand, giving it a light squeeze.

Jessie leans forward and presses her lips to Henry's in a quick kiss, and I glance away during their cutesy moment. She turns her head from his and looks at me. "Bookstore? I want to see my old place of employment, and I want to see Nico."

When I told her Nico and I were together again, I think she

was more excited than I was. For the first week, she kept texting me to send pictures of us together. Most of the time I took a quick picture of us in the apartment and sent it to her. She would act like I just sent her a work of art each time.

We decide to meet at the bookstore after they're checked into their hotel.

Before they leave, I turn back around. "Oh, by the way, Mom's making dinner tonight and wanted to know if you two could come?"

"Please tell me it's lasagna. Please tell me it's lasagna."

I laugh because her hands are clasped together like she's praying. "It's lasagna."

"My prayers have been answered," she cheers to herself.

I shake my head and put my phone back in my bag. Luckily, I don't get lost finding the bus stop back to the parking lot, but I have to wait for about ten minutes before mine arrives.

Me: We're going to stop by the bookstore in a little while. Is that okay?

Nico: It is a public store.

Me: You're in charge. You could deny our entrance.

Nico: Now, why ever would I do that?

Me: Are you smiling right now?

Nico: Maybe?

Me: Me too.

I tuck the phone back in my bag when the bus makes its way to my stop.

Once in my car, instead of going home, I decide to stop by work until Jessie sends me a text letting me know they're on their way.

When I walk inside, I tell the receptionist hello and let her know I'm going to Mom's office.

I walk down the long hallway until I reach Mom. She's absorbed in her work, and I jump through the doorway. "Hey!"

"Geez, May. Are you trying to give me a heart attack?" She has her hand on her chest.

"I wanted to stop by and let you know Jessie and Henry will be over for dinner." I stroll in and take a seat at the chair in front of her desk.

"Great. I remember how lasagna was always her favorite. She'd eat half the casserole dish every time. How was Henry?" Mom straightens up a stack of papers on her desk.

I reach for a pen and twirl it in my fingers. "He's quiet and polite. The opposite of Jessie." I grin.

"Opposites do attract. Well, some of the time. Is Nico coming, too?" She finishes messing with the papers.

"All I said was the word lasagna, and he said he was in." I place the pen back in Mom's jar.

When I told Mom that Nico and I were back together, she was happy about it. Mom was still concerned about me, and she told me even though I was twenty, she still had to go over the whole sex talk again. It was awkward, but I let her so she would feel better.

Mom did start dating Eric, and they're taking things

slowly. He seems good for her. Maybe it will work out or maybe it won't, but at least she's doing what she wants to do.

Mom and I talk until I get Jessie's text.

Jessie: We're leaving now.

Me: See you in a few.

Leaving Mom's office, I drive to the bookstore, and I step out of my car when Jessie and Henry pull into the parking lot.

As we slip inside, Henry walks off to the History section, and Jessie turns to me. "He's a big book fan. Especially history and things like that. I'm usually like, *books?* What are those conspicuous, bright, white pages? Not that all pages are white, but you get the idea."

We walk down a row of books. "But you worked at the bookstore."

"I like the look of books, but I get distracted too easily when I try to read anything more than a chapter." She grips my arm and stops me. "Is that John?"

I spot John, who I saw not too long ago when I brought Nico lunch. He appears more put together than he used to, since he cut all his hair off and dresses a lot better now. He still plays drums, and he and Nico have jam sessions with a few other guys every now and then.

"Yeah, that's him."

"What was I thinking?" she says with a grimace. "He looked so much better before." I don't have a response to that, so I do a weird tilt of my head back.

We talk to John for a few minutes, and he invites Jessie and me to go to a jam session that he has in a couple of weeks.

Jessie tells him she'll be gone with her fiancé by then, but I let him know I'll be there.

"I had to let him know I would be leaving with my fiancé because he was already trying to ask me on a date," Jessie whines, and I laugh.

Some parts of her are still the same and reading John wrong is one of them. He has a girlfriend who he has been dating for years, and Nico said they're very serious.

We find Henry still in the History section with five books in his hands that he plans on purchasing. I leave them there and find Nico in the back, sorting through boxes of books and looks cute doing it.

I press my shoulder against the trim of the door. "Hey."

He turns around and stops what he's doing, giving me a big grin. "You know you can help me if you want."

"For free?" I tease.

"I'll make it up to you." Taking out a stack of books, he sets them by the wall.

"With white chocolate?" My eyes are pleading as I walk to help him unload the box.

"What other way would I be talking about?" His face is full of want as he stands up and backs me into the wall, and I'm not resisting him at all.

"Cheese balls?" Shrugging, I give him an innocent look.

I lean forward, and he meets me halfway with his mouth. I give him a kiss that I meant to be quick, but it immediately escalates into much more time.

"Did I interrupt sexy time?" Jessie's voice calls from the doorway.

We both groan and pull back, but Nico leaves his arms

around my waist.

"Well, we still have our clothes on, so I wouldn't qualify it as sexy time." I brush my hair away from my face.

Jessie turns around and waves Henry in. "Henry, come on, the coast is clear."

Henry strolls in and looks around awkwardly like he heard we were in here naked, which Jessie probably told him that she bet we were in here naked.

We stand around and talk for about an hour, then get ready to leave.

"We'll see you tonight at your mom's," Jessie calls.

"I better get going, too. I'm going to help get the food ready at Mom's house." I've been working with Mom a little on my cooking skills.

I give Nico a hug and start to walk off, and he pulls me backward by the back of my shirt like I knew he would. He gives me a proper kiss goodbye, and my heart inflates.

# Epilogue

Nico told me he had a surprise for me today, and I've been contemplating all day what it could be. I'm pretty sure it has to be food of some kind, because he said he hoped I would be absolutely thrilled.

I'm sitting on our futon in our now shared apartment. We'll eventually buy a couch, but there are too many good memories over the last year. There are permanent dips in the metal frame along the bottom, but those spots now just feel extra comfy like my own little personal nest.

I hear the lock turning, and I leap off the futon and dash toward Nico as he walks in, shutting the door behind him.

Throwing my arms around his neck, I practically slam him into the door as I mold my mouth to his.

"Maybe I should tell you I have a gift for you every day," Nico says as he pulls my body flush with his. Honey-colored eyes meet mine, and I give him a huge grin.

"I think you should." I walk backward to the futon, dragging him along with me while running my hands underneath the back of his shirt, meeting warm skin as I kiss along his jaw and neck.

"You have to stop," he whispers against my ear, but by the

sound of his voice he doesn't want me to quit, and I don't want to either.

Gently, he pulls away from me at the same time the back of my legs strike the futon. Maybe I should drag him to one of the cloud-like recliners. We haven't used one of those for anything besides sitting.

Nico reaches for my chin and turns my face back to his with an auburn eyebrow shooting straight up.

"What?" I ask while laughter escapes me.

"We can go to the chair if you say yes." Nico smiles playfully while stroking the edge of my hand with his thumb.

"Say yes to what?" I search around the room as if there are question marks with hidden answers behind them.

Nico chews on the edge of his lip, looking like he might be shy about something, but then he quickly falls to the floor to one knee—kneeling before me like a knight.

"Do you want me to knight you with a sword, because I will?" I laugh.

His shoulders quake with laughter too as he drags my hand to his chest on top of his heart. The beat is rapid on my palm. "Marry me?"

"Wait, what?" Did he just ask me to marry him? My heart practically stops—then the beats quicken excitedly, and I'm bouncing in my spot.

"Marry me?" He asks again, and his smile is holding hope and maybe a little worry that I will say no, but I would never say no to him. Not about this.

"Yes!" I scream as I drop to the floor, throwing my arms around his neck, knocking him to the carpet.

Pulling us back up, Nico sits me in front of him, both of us on our knees against the soft carpet.

"I don't have a ring." He takes my hand again and strokes circles against my palm.

"I don't need one." The only thing I need is him.

"I didn't know your size, and I wanted it to be a surprise."

"It is!"

Nico slides a hand in his pocket and draws out a piece of red yarn. I stare at it as if it's going to do something amazing, and I think it will.

"This is only temporary until we can size you." Lifting my left hand toward him, he separates my ring finger from the others, and slowly wraps the red string right below my knuckle. With a side grin, he ties the yarn into a bow.

Staring at the string, I smile like it's the greatest gift in the world, and it is.

"I'll never take it off."

"May, I love you." Nico hauls me closer to him.

"I love you, too. Now take me to that chair." I wrap my legs around his waist and my arms around his neck as he lifts me up.

He stumbles all the way to the recliner but makes it there without us crashing to the floor, and I want nothing more than to spend the rest of my life with him.

♥

"I think she's in labor." Nico is on the phone when he opens the door for me. It has been six years since Nico and I got back together, and it still feels like yesterday.

"Are we sure this time?" I can hear Violet's voice on the

other end.

Oh, I hope so! I'm already a week late from my due date. This will be the third time this week that I thought I was in labor. The other times we were sent home.

"We sure hope so, but if not, we'll swing by and see you," Nico says sarcastically.

Hanging up the phone, he gets in the car. I feel the contractions ripple across my back and stomach, and I think I'm going to die. "Hurry!"

"I'm trying." Nico has his hands clenched around the steering wheel.

Violet flew down a week ago and had scheduled the flight around the time of my due date. She probably should've waited until the baby was actually here. She's supposed to fly out in another week to start on a big project and has been endlessly telling me the whole week to get this baby out already. I would if I could.

Nico and I have been married for four years now, and about a year ago, we decided to have a baby. When we discussed kids early on, he told me to tell him whenever I was ready. I finally felt ready, and it only took us a few months.

This time when the pregnancy words showed up on the test, I was thrilled and scared. The entire time I still had thoughts in the back of my mind of what if the same thing happened as before. I have been trying to stay as positive as possible, but I won't feel completely relieved until the baby is nestled in my arms.

I find my phone and send Jessie a text before I forget to later.

Me: The baby is coming. I'll text you a picture after.

Jessie and Henry already have a two-year-old girl and a set of twin boys on the way. She only wanted two kids and was freaking out when she heard the word twins mixed with the word boys. She remembered how her mom always talked about Jessie's twin brothers being wild. That quickly faded into twin boys being the best thing on Earth.

Nico pulls into the hospital, and I want to roll out on the ground and have the baby right here. I don't want to walk anymore, but he helps me inside. One of the workers comes out of nowhere with a wheelchair, and I maneuver myself into it.

The contractions stir, feeling like they are killing me. When we arrive in the hospital room, I climb on the bed while the nurse checks everything, and it's all fine. She calls the doctor, says she's on her way, and that I'll be having the baby soon. If I had the strength to hop out of bed right now and dance, I would.

The nurse leaves the room, and it's only me, Nico, and the pain. "Just think of your happiest moment."

Another wave of pain hits me, and I grit my teeth. "I think my memories have all disappeared."

Nico grabs my hand. "Mine was our wedding day."

"Yeah, that was a great day," I groan and hold onto my stomach. Can this baby come out already?

I try to ignore the agony because the wedding was one of my favorite moments with Nico.

Our wedding was small, and we decided to do it where we first met, which was the bookstore. John got ordained for the occasion, and he stood behind the sell or trade counter. He has even performed other weddings since ours.

Violet had flown down from New York, and Jessie flew in with Henry. Mom was there with Eric at the time, who is now her husband.

Since my dad couldn't walk me down the book aisle, I had my mom walk me instead. I wore a white, casual dress that was lacy and cinched at the waist, hitting right above my knees.

I had put a locket around my neck that Mom let me borrow, and I placed a picture of Dad inside, so he was still with me that day. I painted my nails blue for the something blue, and of course the dress was new.

Violet created me a rose bouquet made from paper—it looked like actual flowers that were bright and spectacular, and I was left speechless.

Nico strummed on his guitar the song from when he first played his instrument for me, and again when he played it through the apartment walls. I walked down the aisle with my arm laced through Mom's, and she was already crying while I was smiling.

Jessie, Henry, and Eric were on one side standing, while Violet, Tim, and Charlotte were on the other.

When Mom released me, I came to stand by Nico, and he set down his guitar, holding my hands in his. The rest of the ceremony was perfect, and I knew I wanted the rest of my life to be spent with Nico.

I feel nostalgic and happy, but then the worst contraction hits me. At the same time, the doctor steps in the room and walks toward me. It's time, and I push when the nurse tells me to, and I think I'm done. I stop, and the nurse tells me to do it again. This happens over and over, and I want to yell at the nurse. Then the doctor finally pulls the baby out and wails echo in the room, filling me with relief.

It's a boy, just as the ultrasound tech told us the baby was going to be. Swaddling him up, the nurse places him in my arms, and he's perfect. He has Nico's mouth and nose, and my brown hair. I turn my head to Nico, who is smiling at the baby and me—his eyes are glistening, and he swipes at them.

This moment is miraculous. I love Nico. I love River Eugene. And I'm going to love our life together, through ups and downs.

**Did you enjoy Hearts Are Like Balloons?**

Authors always appreciate reviews, whether long or short.

**Check out Candace's other books!**

**Wicked Souls Duology**
Vault of Glass
Bride of Glass

**Marked by Magic Duology**
The Bone Valley
Merciless Stars

**Cruel Curses Trilogy**
Clouded By Envy
Veiled By Desire
Shadowed By Despair

**Faeries of Oz Series**
Lion (Short Story Prequel)
Tin
Crow
Ozma
Tik-Tok

**Cursed Hearts Duology**
Lyrics & Curses
Music & Mirrors

**Immortal Letters Duology**
Dearest Clementine: Dark and Romantic Monstrous Tales
Dearest Dorin: A Romantic Ghostly Tale

**Campfire Fantasy Tales**
Lullaby of Flames
A Layer Hidden
The Celebration Game
Mirror, Mirror

**These Vicious Thorns: Tales of the Lovely Grim**
**Between the Quiet**
**Hearts Are Like Balloons**
**Bacon Pie**
**Avocado Bliss**

**Vampires in Wonderland**
Rav (Short Story Prequel)
Maddie
Chess
Knave

**Once Upon A Wicked Villain**
Spindle of Sin

# Acknowledgements

I would like to thank everyone that took a chance at picking up this book to read. One would think contemporary would be easier to write than something fantasy, but for me it wasn't. So, thank you readers.

Thanks to my husband, Nathan, for being one of the most supportive human beings. My daughter, Arwen, you always inspire me to do better.

To my early beta readers, Erika Burden, Patricia Thibodeaux, Kattie Sivley, Victoria Robinson, Brittany Torina, and Mary Frame. I appreciate your guy's advice every time! Rebecca Ayala, thanks for the last-minute saves!

My all-time favorite cover artist, Jenny Zemanek at Seedlings Design Studio. I don't know how you do it, but you managed again to give me exactly what I wanted based on useless notes.

My mom who has always been more dependable than anyone, and to my dad who we miss more than anything.

To anyone that has ever lost anyone important in their life, the best advice I can give is to move forward, but keep the memories alive.

## About the Author

Candace Robinson spends her days consumed by words and hoping to one day find her own DeLorean time machine. Her life consists of avoiding migraines, admiring Bonsai trees, watching classic movies, and living with her husband and daughter in Texas—where it can be forty degrees one day and eighty the next.

## Connect with Candace:

Website: https://authorcandacerobinson.wordpress.com/
Facebook: https://www.facebook.com/literarydust
Twitter: https://twitter.com/literarydust
Instagram:
https://www.instagram.com/candacerobinsonbooks/
Goodreads:
https://www.goodreads.com/author/show/16541001.Candace
_Robinson or ignore that and just try searching for Candace Robinson!